AR

Summer may be coming to a close, but things are still hot enough in the corporate offices on the 17th floor of Connelly Towers, where Drew Connelly has apparently been spending his coffee breaks surfing the Net for a new wife and mother to his young daughter. Inside sources report a "lightning-quick" engagement to a fresh-faced young teacher from Oshkosh whose vital statistics were posted on the Net. And you thought nothing respectable could come from a Web site named "Singlemania."

Chicago plays host once again to Connelly matriarch Miss Lilly, who's visiting from Palm Springs with hubby Tobias—no doubt orchestrating the upcoming nuptials. Instead of matchmaking, the feisty-tempered, eagle-eyed grande dame ought to set her sights on detecting. Seems the troubles at Connelly Corporation continue, and now other family members report further incidents. Scion Grant Connelly's two hired guns have been seen burning the midnight oil and scouring the town for leads into the strange goings-on at the giant corporation. But to date there's been no solution to the mysteries plaguing the venerable family.

Dear Reader,

Dog days of summer got you down? Chill out and relax with six brand-new love stories from Silhouette Desire!

August's MAN OF THE MONTH is the first book in the exciting family-based saga BECKETT'S FORTUNE by Dixie Browning. *Beckett's Cinderella* features a hero honor-bound to repay a generations-old debt and a poor-but-proud heroine leery of love and money she can't believe is offered unconditionally. *His E-Mail Order Wife* by Kristi Gold, in which matchmaking relatives use the Internet to find a high-powered exec a bride, is the latest title in the powerful DYNASTIES: THE CONNELLYS series.

A daughter seeking revenge discovers love instead in *Falling for the Enemy* by Shawna Delacorte. Then, in *Millionaire Cop & Mom-To-Be* by Charlotte Hughes, a jilted, pregnant bride is rescued by her childhood sweetheart.

Passion flares between a family-minded rancher and a marriage-shy divorcée in Kathie DeNosky's *Cowboy Boss*. And a pretend marriage leads to undeniable passion in *Desperado Dad* by Linda Conrad.

So find some shade, grab a cold one…and read all six passionate, powerful and provocative new love stories from Silhouette Desire this month.

Enjoy!

Joan Marlow Golan

Joan Marlow Golan
Senior Editor, Silhouette Desire

Please address questions and book requests to:
Silhouette Reader Service
U.S.: 3010 Walden Ave., P.O. Box 1325, Buffalo, NY 14269
Canadian: P.O. Box 609, Fort Erie, Ont. L2A 5X3

His E-Mail Order Wife

KRISTI GOLD

Published by Silhouette Books

America's Publisher of Contemporary Romance

Special thanks and acknowledgment are given to Kristi Gold for her contribution to the DYNASTIES: THE CONNELLYS series.

Acknowledgments and Dedication
Many thanks to the other Connelly authors for their assistance with this story. And special acknowledgment to all the Drew Connellys of the world who realize that it's the size of a woman's heart that counts.

 SILHOUETTE BOOKS

ISBN 0-373-76454-5

HIS E-MAIL ORDER WIFE

Visit Silhouette at www.eHarlequin.com

Printed in U.S.A.

Books by Kristi Gold

Silhouette Desire

Cowboy For Keeps #1308
Doctor For Keeps #1320
His Sheltering Arms #1350
Her Ardent Sheikh #1358
**Dr. Dangerous* #1415
**Dr. Desirable* #1421
**Dr. Destiny* #1427
His E-Mail Order Wife #1454

*Marrying an M.D.

KRISTI GOLD

began her romance-writing career at the tender age of twelve, when she and her sister spun romantic yarns involving a childhood friend and a popular talk-show host. Since that time, she's given up celebrity heroes for her favorite types of men, doctors and cowboys, as her husband is both. An avid sports fan, she attends football and baseball games in her spare time. She resides on a small ranch in central Texas with her three children and retired neurosurgeon husband, along with various live-stock ranging from Texas longhorn cattle to spoiled yet talented equine. At one time she competed in regional and national Appaloosa horse shows as a nonpro, but gave up riding for writing and turned the reins over to her youngest daughter. She attributes much of her success to her sister, Kim, who encouraged her in her writing, even during the tough times. When she's not in her office writing her current book, she's dreaming about it. Readers may contact Kristi at P.O. Box 11292, Robinson, TX 76716.

MEET THE CONNELLYS

Meet the Connellys of Chicago—
wealthy, powerful and rocked by scandal,
betrayal...and passion!

Who's Who in
HIS E-MAIL ORDER WIFE

Drew Connelly—He thinks of himself as a widowed
single dad/corporate VP who's too harried to arrange
even dinner and a movie. To the rest of the world, he's
sexy, successful and *so* available....

Kristina Simmons—She thinks of herself as full-figured,
the kind of woman with a "nice personality." *Desirable*
has never been a term to describe her...until she sees
herself reflected in Drew's eyes....

Lilly Connelly—Don't let the cane and the old birth
certificate fool you. Nothing gets past the Connelly
matriarch. But does she see *everything?*

Prologue

"Is she really coming, Nana Lilly?"

Lilly hugged her cherished great-granddaughter securely against her chest as they sat before the computer. "Yes, Amanda, she's really coming."

Lilly Connelly was an old dog short on new tricks, at one time believing the almighty Internet was the spawn of the devil. But she'd recently found that surfing the Net was pretty darned nifty at that, especially when she discovered Chicago's latest matchmaking website, a place to scan prospective young women looking for male companionship. Much like a high-tech coming-out party minus the caterer.

As far as Lilly was concerned, one young woman definitely fit the bill for the perfect wife for her grandson, Drew, and a suitable mother for his little Amanda. This particular candidate loved children, logical since she was a Montessori teacher—and also wanted a steady relationship and marriage. She was a far cry from the succession of women who had marched through Drew's life for the past five years since his wife's death, women who only had designs on his fortune and all the status that came with the Connelly name.

Darn that Drew, Lilly thought. He didn't know what was good for him. Fortunately, she did. Still, he was a considerate man and an excellent father. Oh, he might be a trifle mad when he learned what she had done. But if luck prevailed, he'd come to realize that grandmother always knows best.

Lilly pressed the send button on the final e-mail, setting in motion a plan that had been weeks in the making. This should probably be the moment Lilly felt a little nip of guilt, but she didn't. The Connellys were a stubborn lot; Drew was no exception. He needed a little push, something Lilly was more than happy to provide, with or without the benefit of her cane.

She brushed a kiss across Amanda's cheek and gave her a gentle nudge. "Hop down, dear heart. I have to go now. Grandpa Toby's expecting me home soon."

Amanda scooted off Lilly's lap and swiveled the office chair so that Lilly could stand. Lilly grasped the cane and rose on uncooperative legs, her eighty-three-year-old joints groaning in protest. She'd been sitting too long, and she was too creaky to stay in the same position for minutes, much less hours.

Looking down on sweet, sweet Amanda's trusting green eyes so full of hope, the guilt finally hit Lilly full-force. Had she done the right thing? Entirely too late to turn back now.

Lilly wished she could kneel at Amanda's level but she might never get up if she did. She settled for touching the top of Amanda's head covered in fine white-blond hair. "Dear, you realize this might not work between your father and Kristina, don't you?"

"It will work," Amanda said adamantly, topped off by a determined jut of her chin. "She'll love my daddy, and my daddy will love her, too."

Lilly's heart took a little tumble. Although Amanda might look like her mother—God rest poor Talia's misguided soul—she had her father's tenacity. Luckily she'd been blessed with Lilly's optimism. "We'll hope your daddy and Kristina get along, but I want you to know that sometimes adults don't see eye to eye on things. We also have to keep this our little secret for a while." And, she hoped, by the time Kristina Simmons did learn the truth, all would be settled with love.

"Kristina says she likes puppies," Amanda replied as if she refused to consider the possibility that the arrangement wouldn't work. "Maybe she'll talk Daddy into getting me one."

"One step at a time, dear. She has to meet your daddy first." And convince him to let her stay.

Lilly prayed she had, indeed, done the right thing. Prayed that Drew would give the young woman a chance. Prayed that Kristina Simmons possessed a strong heart and the ability to heal Drew's shattered one.

One could always hope that that would be the case.

One

Drew Connelly dropped his bags at the bottom of the staircase leading to the second floor—and landed the largest on his foot. He muttered a string of curses directed at his stupidity, the late hour, the sound of the nanny's grating voice coming from the kitchen while she gabbed on the phone with God only knew who.

When Mrs. Parker had abruptly left his employ to move in with her ailing daughter out of state, Drew had been desperate. The agency had sent him Debbie Randles, a young au pair with minimal experience. One week in her presence and he'd had his doubts about her abilities, but because of urgent business in Europe, he'd had no choice.

At least he'd been assured that his grandmother would stop by to check on Amanda daily. Thankfully nothing out of the ordinary had happened during his absence.

After the weekend, he'd contact the agency again and

demand that they find him a suitable replacement, someone a little older with more experience. Someone who liked Amanda, and whom Amanda liked.

God, how he'd missed his daughter. A month was entirely too long to be away from her. The daily phone calls had been sorry replacements for seeing her vibrant smile, hearing her contagious laughter. He recalled their last conversation in which she'd told him she had a surprise for him. At least the nanny had followed one of his mandates—bedtime for Amanda no later than 10:00 p.m. since it was summer—otherwise he would have been greeted by his squealing six-year-old, a bundle of energy and joy wrapped up in one delicate dynamite package. The very light of his life, and the reason why he got up every morning to face his grueling schedule as Vice President of Overseas Operations for Connelly Corporation, his family's legacy.

Unfortunately, the responsibility was rapidly aging him. Tonight he felt two hundred years old, not twenty-seven.

Trudging up the stairs, Drew planned to go immediately to Mandy's room and kiss her good-night, take a quick shower, then pass out in bed. But he stopped short when he heard a giggle coming from his second-floor study. Amanda's giggle.

So much for his daughter being tucked soundly into bed. Yeah, he had to find another nanny, and soon.

Drew dropped his bags once again, this time avoiding his toes, and strode down the hallway and into the office to find Amanda perched on her knees in his chair, her face lit by the glow of the computer screen and sheer amusement.

"Young lady, you're supposed to be in bed," he said with all the sternness he could muster.

"Daddy! You're home!" Amanda climbed out of the chair and rushed him like a tiny tornado. Drew hoisted her up in his arms, relishing the clean scent of her hair, her soft cheek resting against his evening-shadowed jaw, her fragile frame curled against his chest. Little did his baby girl know she had his heart so securely tied around her little finger he could never stay mad at her for any length of time. Then again, she probably did know.

After he hugged her hard and kissed her cheek, she pulled back and studied him with green eyes bright with excitement. "Daddy, I missed you so bad!"

"I missed you too, sweetheart, but we need to talk about the computer." He attempted to look serious, sound serious, a difficult thing to do with Amanda smiling at him. "Haven't I told you that you're not supposed to be on the Internet unless an adult is with you? It's dangerous, Mandy."

"I know, Daddy." She began to play with his tie, avoiding his scrutiny. "But Nana Lilly was with me." She looked up and nailed him with another luminous grin. "I showed her how to use the computer."

A miracle in itself. His grandmother normally had to be dragged kicking and screaming into the new world. "But she's not here now, is she? Which means you've disobeyed me."

Amanda's lip puckered and Drew's heart began to hurt. "Debbie was with me until a few minutes ago, Daddy. We were surfing together."

That provided little relief for Drew. "Visiting your favorite animal site?"

"I helped her pick out a man."

Obviously he'd underestimated the nanny's poor judgment. "What do you mean you picked out a man?"

"On Singlemania."

"Singlemania?"

"The same place we got your surprise."

The scenario was getting more and more bizarre. "My surprise?"

His daughter's face once again brightened. "The surprise I told you about on the phone, silly Daddy. It will be here in the morning."

Drew sensed certain disaster. "Debbie helped you with this surprise?"

"Debbie showed me and Nana the website. Nana helped me get you the surprise."

Great. Just great. He couldn't imagine anything of merit to be found on a singles' site. His grandmother could be way out there at times, but she wouldn't subject Amanda to anything kinky. Still, Drew didn't have a clue what Lilly had done. He wasn't sure he wanted to know, but he had to find out. "What kind of surprise did you and Nana come up with?"

She looked away again. "I'm not supposed to tell you 'cause then it won't be a surprise."

"Ah, come on, Mandy," he cajoled. "Just a little hint. I won't tell Nana you told me."

Amanda tipped up her chin with pride, beamed like a billboard and proudly announced, "We got you a wife."

"Get off the phone, Ms. Randles. Now."

Kicked back in a chair in the kitchen, Debbie stared up at Drew, the cordless phone tucked between her jaw and shoulder while she filed her nails. "I'll call you back, Henry."

She dropped the nail file and phone onto the table and her feet from the chair across from her then came to attention. "Uh, Mr. Connelly, I didn't know you were home."

"No kidding."

"Is there something wrong?"

Drew released a humorless bark of a laugh. "You could say that. Amanda tells me she's been getting quite an education on your singles' site. Seems she helped you pick out a man." And in turn helped his grandmother select him a wife.

"I was only checking out some profiles and getting her opinion."

"And you think this is proper for my daughter?"

"I don't think she's been damaged by the experience."

Drew lost any semblance of calm. "She's six years old, dammit."

The nanny had the nerve to look innocent. "It's never too early to learn good skills in the singles world."

"You're fired."

Her eyes went saucer wide. "What?"

"You heard me. Get your things and get out of here. I'll send your final check to the agency."

"It's after midnight."

Drew realized that was true, and he couldn't very well put her out in the streets this time of night. "Then I want you out first thing in the morning. I'll have my company driver pick you up and take you wherever you want to go."

"Please, Mr. Connelly," she pleaded. "I can't go live with my mother again. She'll drive me crazy."

Drew was already halfway there so she might as well join him. "I'm sorry, Ms. Randles, but that's your problem. You should have thought about that when you turned my daughter loose on the Internet." And subsequently his grandmother.

He spun around and headed back up the stairs, leaving the nanny alone with her mouth gaping. In the hallway, he headed toward Amanda's room to make sure she was still in bed where he'd left her a few moments before.

While he'd tucked her in bed, he'd told his daughter that no matter what transpired between him and the mysterious Kristina the following morning, the circumstances behind their meeting—the e-mails and his grandmother's scheming—shouldn't be revealed because he didn't want to hurt the lady's feelings. And Drew sincerely didn't want to do that regardless of the fact he knew nothing about her. As far as he was concerned, Kristina Simmons had been an innocent victim in this whole bizarre mess.

Mandy had assured Drew they would keep it "their own little secret" and promised she wouldn't say anything to "hurt *her* Kristina's feelings." Drew felt somewhat satisfied, yet he couldn't trust that Mandy wouldn't innocently spill the beans. All the more reason to find some way to gently tell Kristina the truth, then send her on her way.

Through the partially open door of Mandy's room, Drew found her asleep, her angelic face turned toward him, her eyes closed against the hall light. She looked like a pint-size princess—like her mother. He certainly didn't need to think about her now.

In his room, Drew collapsed onto the bed and grabbed the phone, hitting the speed dial. One task down, one to go.

"H'lo."

"Grandfather, it's Drew. Is Grandmother there?"

"Good grief, son, do you know what time it is?"

"I know, but this can't wait."

"Is something wrong?"

Oh, yeah, thanks to thoroughly meddling Lilly. "I just need to talk to her. Is she asleep?"

"No. She's in the other room watching late-night talk shows. The ones that turn into a free-for-all."

Not surprising to Drew. Lilly was into high drama. "Can you get her for me?"

"Certainly, son. Lilly, it's Drew!"

Drew held the phone away, fearing his grandfather's booming voice might burst an eardrum. That would be all he needed tonight.

"Hello, Drew," Lilly said in her sweet-as-sugar voice that indicated she was up to no good. "Did you have a nice trip?"

"Did you have fun playing on my computer?"

"Oh, yes, dear. That Amanda is quite a little whiz—"

"Cut the crap, Grandmother."

"I beg your pardon?"

"I know what you've done."

"Now, simmer down, young man. I've done you a favor."

"A favor?" Drew's ears began to burn and ring simultaneously. "Did you really think I'd want you setting me up with some woman I don't even know? I'm not interested in going on a blind date!"

"It's not a date, dear."

"Call it what you will, but I don't enjoy the thought of some stranger showing up at my doorstep expecting to meet me in the morning after I've been up most of the night."

"She won't be there to meet you."

"Stop talking in riddles, Lilly."

"She'll be there to move in with you."

His arrival from Europe into the Twilight Zone was now complete. "You're kidding, right?"

"No. For your information, you've been e-mailing her

for the month you were away. So has Amanda. Her name is Kristina Simmons—a nice name, don't you think?''

Nothing about this was nice. "Dammit, Lilly, this is insane!''

"Don't curse me, young man.''

He cursed the fact that he'd come home to find this mess. "Just what do you really know about her?''

"She seems to be a very cordial—''

"Cordial? What if she's a criminal, for God's sake? How could you invite some stranger into my home?''

"Stop interrupting and I will provide all the details necessary for you to give her a proper welcome.'' Lilly paused to catch a breath. "I've had her checked out thoroughly, and she's a model citizen, as I suspected from her correspondence. Amanda helped me write all the e-mails. Very harmless, really. And of course, you've recently proposed, the only fitting thing to do with a child in the house and your reputation at stake. It will be a trial engagement of a month, and after that time, if all goes well—which it will—you will make the wedding plans. Kristina need never know the truth.''

This was so absurd. So surreal. So Lilly. "Grandmother, I don't know what century you think this is, but arranged marriages went out with potbellied stoves.''

"This is for your own good, Drew. For Amanda's own good. I can no longer stand by and watch your child being raised by a succession of hapless nannies while you travel about the world and date floozies who only want to get into your pants as well as your pocketbook.''

Nothing Lilly had done to this point shocked Drew more than her current scheme, and her low opinion of his social life. Didn't she realize how much he hated leaving Amanda because his job demanded he spend time out of the country? Hated the whole dating scene because not one woman measured up to his ideal, both as a wife for him and mother for his child? Hated that his grandmother saw fit to remedy that situation by finding him a bride? "You can't play me like this, Grandmother."

"I already have, my beloved, lonely grandson. And being the gentleman that you are, you will welcome this woman with open arms and give her a chance."

"And if I don't?"

"You will have to answer to me, a fate worse than hell."

With that the line went dead, but Drew's temper was alive and well, hovering close to the boiling point.

What was he going to do now? Hope that the mysterious Kristina wouldn't show up? That she'd bow out graciously, maybe even laugh once she learned this was some stunt executed by a matchmaking matriarch? One way or the other, he would let her know point-blank that this whole setup was one huge mistake.

Sitting in her car at the curb in front of Drew Connelly's impressive Chicago residence, Kristina Simmons was beginning to wonder if she'd made a colossal mistake.

When her friend Tori had proposed putting Kristina's profile and photo on the singles site, Kristina had balked. Despite her objections, and without her knowledge, Tori had put them up anyway. Then came the e-mails from Drew Connelly that she'd originally intended to ignore. But she hadn't been able to ignore those sent by his daughter, Amanda.

As it turned out, Drew was a very interesting correspondent, and Kristina found herself being drawn in by his words, by his daughter. Yet never in her wildest imaginings had she believed she would actually meet someone over the Internet, much less agree to a trial *engagement* to that someone. It still wasn't too late to change her mind.

Then she glanced at the copy of the e-mail attached to the bottom of the directions lying on the passenger seat.

dear Kristina.
i cant wait to see you in the morning. you are pretty and you look like a mommy. daddy needs a wife bad. if you come i promis i will be good.

love, Amanda.

How could she refuse a child's heartfelt plea? Okay, so maybe somewhere deep inside she clung to the hope that Amanda's father might be the man of her dreams. He seemed so nice in the e-mails, so much like her, a lonely person searching for a meaningful relationship. She could relate to that loneliness, the pitfalls of single life. Though she was barely twenty-seven, she had already grown tired of sorting through the dating chaos, encountering those armed with questionable intentions and pretty lies. Now she had agreed to reside with a man she didn't know beyond e-mail correspondence.

Temporarily reside with him, Kristina corrected. If it didn't work out, she would simply walk away, though she'd probably not return to her native Wisconsin. As long as she didn't do something stupid—like fall madly in love with Drew Connelly if there wasn't any indication he could love her back—this shouldn't be a problem. But if he was anything at all like the man behind the e-mails, admittedly she was already a little bit in love with him.

Sliding out of the car, Kristina grabbed only her tote bag, opting to leave her suitcases in the trunk, and headed up the sidewalk, fear following close behind. Did she really want to do this?

She hadn't really done anything yet other than agree to live in Drew's home on a trial basis. And there was that little matter of conducting a background search on Drew Connelly to see if he was legitimate, including having Tori's policeman friend make certain he had no criminal history. He was more than legitimate—a wealthy man who'd grown up in a powerful, renowned Chicago family, proverbial pillars of the community. He enjoyed a great deal of success, judging from the size of his house, a beautiful red-brick home with neatly manicured grounds and gardens, situated in a prosperous neighborhood.

Once on the porch, Kristina pressed the bell before she could change her mind. She waited an excruciating amount of time for someone to answer her summons. Her heart pounded in her chest and her palms began to perspire.

If only she'd seen a picture of him, not that his physical appearance would sway her one way or the other. Lord knew men had judged her on that issue one too many times. Though she'd learned to deal with her above-average height, her practically non-existent waistline, her more-than-ample hips and breasts, at times throughout her life she'd longed for a different body type. But she'd stopped wishing for something that could never be and found comfort in knowing that maybe someone might accept her for who she was inside instead of what she wasn't outside. Maybe that someone was Drew Connelly. Regardless of what he looked like, Kristina refused to be anything but pleasant. After all, the man beneath the facade was all that counted. Looks didn't matter.

The door opened to a stout man dressed in a flannel

shirt and khaki slacks, slightly balding, not very tall, and if he was twenty-seven years old, then she was a size six.

At least his smile was warm, cheerful. "Good morning, missy. Can I help you?"

Kristina sent him an answering smile, a shaky one. "Is this the Connelly residence?"

"Yes, ma'am. Are you from the agency?"

"The agency?"

"The nanny service."

Nanny service? "Uh, well, no. I'm supposed to be meeting with Drew Connelly. Is that you?"

His laugh was loud, buoyant. "I wish, but I'm afraid I'm a little longer in the tooth than Drew." He stuck out his hand. "I'm Tobias Connelly, Drew's grandfather."

Kristina took his hand for a quick, robust shake, admittedly relieved. "I'm Kristina Simmons."

"Nice to meet you, Miss— Is it Miss?"

Obviously the man knew nothing about the engagement, and Kristina thought it best not to make him any the wiser. "Yes, it's Miss."

"Well, Miss Simmons, is Drew expecting you?"

"I think so." She hoped so.

He opened the door wide and gestured her inside. "Come on in then."

What Kristina encountered in the foyer took her breath away. A staircase with a highly polished banister climbed upward toward the second floor. To her right, a formal living room displayed exquisite furniture, priceless antiques, she would guess. To her left, a library housed shelves full of books and comfortable leather sofas. Before her, a long entry hall with gleaming slate-colored ceramic tile seemed to stretch for miles.

The place was all opulent elegance, polished to perfection. The home most dreams were made of.

So what in the heck was she doing here, plain Kristina Simmons from Oshkosh?

Tobias yelled, "Drew, you have company!" startling Kristina.

"I'll be there in a minute!" an irritable masculine voice called back.

The elder Connelly chuckled. "He's having his coffee. You don't want to deal with him until he does. He can be a real bear in the morning."

Oh, wonderful. A man who didn't do mornings, Kristina's favorite time of day. "I see."

"Do you want me to show you to the kitchen?"

"No!" She hadn't meant to sound so panicked, but she felt it best to stay near the exit in case she needed a quick escape. "I mean, I'll just wait for him here."

"Would you like to have a seat?" He indicated the formal furniture in the adjacent living room. It looked nice, but not all that comfortable.

"I'm fine, really."

"Okay. I'm sure he'll be here in a minute."

Another minute might not be enough time for Kristina to prepare, especially for a bear.

Tobias sent her a questioning look as if trying to read her thoughts, uncover her secrets. "I should've known you weren't from the agency," he said. "You're not at all what they sent the last time, some skinny young thing with barely a brain in her head."

Kristina was definitely not skinny, and not brainless under normal circumstances, though at the moment she questioned her wisdom. Obviously Drew Connelly was without a nanny. Could this be the reason behind his request for her to move in? "Then I assume he's looking for someone to take care of Amanda."

"As of early this morning. He had to fire the latest

one because she wasn't doing her job. Another reason why he's in such a foul mood.''

That relieved Kristina somewhat. At least it appeared he hadn't brought her here solely to replace his nanny.

Tobias grinned. "I'm sure he'll be much better now that you're here. Nothing like a pretty girl to brighten a young man's morning.''

A pretty girl? "Thanks," she muttered, realizing he was probably only being polite, a good trait, one she hoped he'd instilled in his grandson.

Tobias glanced at his watch then regarded her with kind eyes. "I hate to have to part good company, but I was just on my way out. Every now and then I need to check on the boy, make sure he's staying in line." He opened the front door and sent her another cheery smile. "Take care, Miss Simmons. I hope we see each other again soon. Have Drew bring you around some time. I know his grandmother would love to meet you.''

With that he was out the door, leaving Kristina alone to wait for the mysterious Drew Connelly.

On wobbly knees, she turned to one of the windows framing the front door and surveyed the surroundings outside. Drenched in the mid-August sun, a beautiful parkway sporting benches and lush lawns split the street, a lovely place for kids to play under the watchful eyes of their parents. Kristina wished she could abandon her shoes and play at the moment, but no matter how tempting that thought, she couldn't run away now.

She kneaded her clammy hands, wondering what Drew Connelly was really like. A younger version of his grandfather, maybe. Kind and considerate, once he had his caffeine. But what would he think of her? Drew had said in his e-mails that appearance didn't matter. Still, after he saw all of her, not just a head-shot photo, he could very well change his mind.

The sound of footsteps on tiled floor echoed behind her, signaling that the moment of truth had arrived.

Straightening her shoulders, Kristina turned and stifled a gasp at the man coming toward her—a gorgeous man wearing a gaping navy robe that revealed a spattering of dark hair on a well-defined chest and a pair of low-riding pajama bottoms that showcased his board-flat belly. He stopped for a minute then continued on more slowly before halting a scant few feet away.

Kristina actually had to look up at him, an uncommon occurrence considering her height. His narrowed eyes were shockingly blue, his mussed wavy hair raven black. He looked entirely too sexy, as if he'd just crawled out of bed.

Just crawled out of bed?

Heavens, had he forgotten she was coming? Had she got the time wrong? Was this really him?

"Drew?"

His gaze roamed lazily over her, from forehead to feet, then settled on her eyes. "You must be Kristina," he said in a low, husky voice.

At the moment she wasn't sure who she was, or if she could clear away the shock, both from his appearance and his steady perusal, in order to speak. "Yes, I'm Kristina. Am I early?" *Am I crazy?*

"It's barely 8:00 a.m. I think that would qualify as early, especially on a Saturday."

"That's what time you told me to be here."

He frowned. "I did?"

"Yes. I have it right here." She rummaged through the nylon tote thrown over her shoulder to retrieve the final e-mail. "It says, 'Come at 8:00 a.m. We can talk before Amanda wakes up.''' She shoved the paper back into her bag and when he didn't respond, she added, "Do you want me to come back later?" *Or maybe never?*

"Kristina! You came!"

Kristina turned to find a flaxen-haired little girl wearing a pink satin nightgown, bounding down the stairs as fast as her tiny feet would allow. Once she reached the bottom, she kept going and hurled herself at Kristina's legs, nearly knocking Kristina backward in the process.

She knelt and smiled, her hands braced on the little girl's thin shoulders. "Let me guess. You must be the maid."

She giggled and squirmed. "I'm Amanda. You can call me Mandy like my daddy if you want."

One innocent smile from this beautiful child, and Kristina was already in love. "I'd like to call you Mandy, if it's okay with your daddy."

Kristina glanced up to find Drew hovering over them, looking less than pleased. "Mandy, why don't you go upstairs so I can talk to Kristina alone?"

Amanda stuck out her lip in a practiced pout. "I wanna talk to her, too."

"Later, Amanda Elizabeth."

When Amanda hung her head and looked as though she might cry, Kristina gave her a quick hug. "Tell you what, sweetie. Why don't you go up and get dressed, then find me some of your favorite toys? I can come up and see you in a little while."

"Promise?"

"I promise."

"You're not going to go away?"

Kristina's heart squeezed tightly in her chest. Obviously Amanda had been left before, maybe often. Maybe her father was one to bring women into their life then push them away as soon as Amanda got close to them. Maybe this was a bad idea.

She straightened and said, "I won't go away right now." It was all that Kristina could promise at the moment, since the decision now rested on Drew. "I'll come up as soon as your dad and I are finished talking."

Amanda looked wary, disappointed. "Okay." She trudged back up the stairs, looking over her shoulder now and then, probably to see if Kristina would keep her promise.

Once the little girl was out of sight, Kristina turned back to Drew. He'd cinched his robe, covering his chest completely, but he looked no less attractive and no less uncomfortable.

He studied the ceiling for a moment before bringing his gaze back to her. "Look, Kristina, there's something I need to say to you."

Considering his serious tone, Kristina had no doubt what he was going to say. After taking one look at her, he'd probably changed his mind. So much for appearance not counting.

She glanced at the staircase and found it empty. Still, she didn't want Amanda to overhear the dismissal. "Is there some place more private where we can talk?"

"Sure. Right this way."

Kristina followed Drew Connelly down the lengthy corridor, preparing for the moment when he told her this was one huge mistake.

Two

Drew wouldn't have been more surprised if Lilly had driven up on a Harley. He didn't know what he'd been expecting of Kristina Simmons, but this wasn't it.

She settled on the sofa in the den; he took the lounge chair across from her. Avoiding his gaze, she surveyed the silent room, allowing him to assess her unassuming attire of plain white sandals and sleeveless coral dress that revealed not much more than arms and ankles. Her skin was bronze in coloring, surprising, considering her long dark auburn hair. She was tall, probably close to six feet, and nothing at all like the women he usually dated.

Kristina Simmons was a throwback to a time when women were women, with ample breasts and generous curves that left no doubt about their gender. However, she tried to conceal those attributes behind loose-fitting clothes, probably because that look was no longer in vogue, thanks to the assumption that a woman had to be emaciated to be attractive. But Drew could imagine every fine detail. Man, could he imagine, and he needed to stop doing that immediately before he embarrassed himself.

Kristina's big brown eyes proved to be one of her most notable features, eyes that had frozen him in his tracks when he'd first seen her standing in his foyer. Eyes that assessed him now and then while he considered what he needed to say.

"Did you have any trouble finding the house?" Lame, but he couldn't think of anything beyond small talk at the moment, especially when his gaze kept drifting to her full lips.

"Not at all. You give great directions." Her sudden smile revealed white teeth that contrasted with her golden coloring. It was also wan, self-conscious. "Your house is beautiful. So is your daughter."

So was Kristina Simmons, in a natural, unsullied way, Drew decided. She didn't wear much makeup. She didn't have to. Her skin was flawless, her lashes thick and long, fanning against her cheeks when she lowered her eyes, as she did at that moment.

"Mandy's a great kid," he said. "Precocious, I guess you could say."

"Intelligent, I'd say." She grabbed up the decorative pillow next to her and hugged it to her chest, her eyes fixed on some focal point to her right. "Okay, so what did you want to tell me?"

He knew what he needed to tell her—this whole ridiculous scheme had been masterminded by his grandmother. But the way Kristina looked at the moment, unsure and circumspect, he didn't have the heart to blurt out the revelation. He'd have to ease into it gradually. "I think we should talk about this arrangement."

She tossed the pillow aside and scooted to the edge of

the sofa, her hands clasped tightly in her lap, and met his gaze head-on. "Look, I'll make this easy on you. I realize you're surprised by my appearance, and I know you said in your e-mails that it didn't matter. But I can certainly understand why you might not find me suitable."

"What's that supposed to mean?"

"Well, a good-looking rich guy like you could have any woman he pleases. A woman who would be, shall we call it, more svelte, delicate. Thin."

That didn't set well with Drew. Inaccurate assumptions about him never did. "Do you really think I'm that superficial?"

"I really don't know what to think. I wasn't exactly expecting you."

That made two of them. He hadn't counted on her either, a woman who had his imagination working overtime. "What were you expecting?"

"Honestly?"

"I think that's probably best." Although he had yet to be honest with her.

"I was expecting someone a little more—"

"Homely?"

"Plain."

"So was I."

A slight splotch of pink colored her cheeks and she grabbed the pillow again. "At least one of us wasn't wrong."

How could she say that? Didn't she realize that she had a simple beauty a man would have to be dead not to notice? Not to mention she'd made a connection with Mandy immediately. How many times had he hoped to see that happen with any of the women he'd introduced to his daughter? More times than he could count, and it hadn't happened—until now. Maybe Lilly was right.

Maybe he'd been looking in the wrong places. But the Internet?

Regardless, he had no intention of getting caught in the matrimony trap any time soon. He'd tried that once and it had been one of the most devastating experiences of his life. Amanda was the only good thing to come out of it.

But how could he tell Kristina Simmons that he wasn't interested without making it seem as though her looks had something to do with it? How could he explain it to his daughter, who had looked at Kristina with open worship, without destroying her completely?

Damn Lilly for putting him in this predicament without regard to Amanda's feelings. Or Kristina's. If he sent Kristina on her way now, he might lead her to believe that he was as superficial as she'd assumed. Not to mention he'd have to deal with his grandmother's and his daughter's wrath. Now what was he going to do?

Then something occurred to him. Maybe he could subtly convince Kristina that this wasn't going to work out. Maybe he could totally turn her off, let it be her idea to leave. That was a better plan. A great plan.

First, he'd start with a leer. God knew he'd seen it done enough times in the office when one of the male staff members had the hots for one of the secretaries. If that didn't scare her off, then she was a lot tougher than he'd presumed. "Well, Kristina, I think you're an exceedingly attractive woman." Hell, he sounded like a bad impression of Dudley Watts, Connelly Corporation's resident lecher.

Unfortunately, Kristina found the fringe on the pillow more interesting than his attempt at being seedy. "Thank you."

"And I'm looking forward to us getting to know each

other *better*." At least he sounded a little more suave. Less Dudley, anyway.

She glanced up from the pillow, surprise in her expression. "Then you're saying we should go ahead with this arrangement?"

"Unless that's a problem for you?"

Her gaze faltered once again. "No. I agreed to do this, and I think we should give it a try."

So much for his first attempts to discourage her. He would just have to try harder to convince her that he had questionable intentions. "Do you need help moving your things?"

"Everything I own is in my car."

"You've been living in your car?"

That earned Drew a smile. "Not hardly. My lease ran out on my apartment this week, so when you asked me to move in, I decided not to renew. I guess you could say that this couldn't have come at a better time."

Now Drew felt even worse. If he put her out, she'd be—for all intents and purposes—homeless. Back to plan A—dubious overtures. He leaned forward and attempted a come-on look, although his face felt stiff with the effort. "I think you'll find my bed more than comfortable."

She leaned forward, too, seeming oddly relaxed. "Really, Drew, you don't have to give up your room. As I told you before, the guest room will be fine."

He sat back. "You think we should have separate bedrooms?"

"Of course, exactly what you proposed in the e-mail. I agree with you that we shouldn't even consider that kind of intimacy with Amanda living in the house."

Lilly had obviously set him up for sainthood. If he told Kristina he'd changed his mind, that he wanted her in his bed—not exactly an unappealing thought—then he'd definitely look like a class-A jackass. He couldn't go quite that far...yet. "Just checking to see if we're on the same page with this."

"We are," she said. "I believe we need a lot more time before taking that step in our relationship."

So much for plan A. "Tell me more about yourself," he said in hopes of coming upon something else to convince her to steer clear of him.

"I'm not sure what I can say that I haven't said in my e-mails."

Drew realized she had a definite advantage there. "I'm sure you can think of something. You can't know everything about someone in a few e-mails."

"We exchanged fifty."

Fifty? His grandmother seriously needed to find another hobby. "That many, huh?"

"Yes, I counted them. I also kept them."

Drew made a mental note to try and retrieve them from his inbox later, if Lilly hadn't destroyed the evidence of her deceitful doings. "Which was your favorite e-mail?"

Her great smile traveled all the way to her coffee-colored eyes. "Let me think. I believe it's the one where you told me one of your favorite books was *Wuthering Heights*."

"I bet that surprised you." Sure as hell surprised him since he'd never read the book. But Lilly had. His grandmother knew no shame.

"To be honest," Kristina continued, "I think Heathcliff was a bit too tortured."

Heathcliff had nothing on Drew at the moment. "He was, uh, unique."

"And tortured. That's why I'm surprised you also like romantic comedies."

Drew nearly choked on that one, yet it also led to another idea. Maybe if he could convince her that he hadn't been forthcoming with the truth about his tastes, she'd decide to leave immediately. "Actually, I was only trying to impress you. I really prefer Tom Clancy."

Her grin widened. "Really? So do I. I love military thrillers."

So much for that strategy. "Did I tell you that I like sports?"

"No, we didn't discuss that."

Finally, something to work with. "Well, I do. Friday through Sunday when I'm home. Whatever's on the tube. But my favorite is wrestling." That ought to do it.

It didn't. Kristina looked pleased, excited even. "I am so glad to hear that. I adore wrestling. The Mangler is my favorite. Don't you just love that crazy hat he wears? And when he takes on that woman, what's her name?"

Drew had no clue. He'd never watched wrestling, either. "I can't remember at the moment. I'm still pretty jet-lagged."

Kristina's dark brows drew down into a frown. "Jet-lagged? I didn't know you've been out of town."

"Europe. For the past month."

"You sent all those e-mails from Europe?"

"Yeah, I did."

The lies were getting deeper and deeper. If Drew knew what was good for him, for her, he'd put a stop to this now. He'd tell Kristina the truth. He'd quit staring at her dark eyes, her fingers dancing over the pillow, her tempting lips now parted in surprise, and just blurt it out.

Then she added, "That's so sweet, Drew. I had no idea. Surely that cost you quite a bit of money, connecting to the Internet in Europe. You shouldn't have gone to all that trouble for me."

She sounded as if he'd sent her a Monet, not an e-mail. How could he tell her the truth now? He couldn't.

Besides, after seeing the nanny off at dawn with good riddance, he had no one to care for his daughter. It might take the better part of a month to find a decent replacement. Kristina was obviously good with kids, and Amanda liked her. In the meantime, he could pretend he was going along with this arrangement and try to come up with more ways to discourage her. Simple enough, except for one minor problem: He was more than a little attracted to her. However, he didn't intend to let that deter him from his goal.

Standing, he said, "Let's get you settled in."

Kristina rose from the sofa, spanned the distance between them, and drew him into an unexpected hug. Her full breasts pressed against his chest. She smelled fresh, clean, felt warm against him. Good. Too good. His hands traveled to the dip at her spine. It took all his strength not to travel lower, mold his hands to her hips, pull her closer, kiss her thoroughly.

Then she said, "Thanks, Drew," in a silky voice, deep and slightly raspy. Drew immediately reacted to the sound, becoming steel-hard below his belt, and he wondered what she would sound like when he made love to her.

When he made love to her?

He quickly stepped back, out of her inviting embrace, away from dangerous thoughts. He had no business entertaining those fantasies, not if he wanted to put an end to this charade. He had to be strong, keep his hands and mouth to himself. No problem. He could do that.

"Let me show you to bed, Kristina." Damn. "Your bedroom, I mean."

* * *

After settling in to the guest quarters downstairs, a rose-colored suite straight out of a designer's dream, Kristina sat cross-legged on the floor in Amanda's lavender, frill-filled room surrounded by enough toys to stock a department store. She and Amanda were dressing two fashion dolls while Drew showered and dressed in the room down the hall, something Kristina dared not think about.

Not after that hug. Not after her unexpected reaction to Drew Connelly's arms wrapped around her.

For the first time in years, she'd experienced true chemistry. And she couldn't help but think Drew had experienced it, too. Or at least she thought he had.

Heaven help her, one innocuous hug and she was already considering things she had no cause to consider. Not until they knew each other better. Then whatever happened, happened. Still, she couldn't stop thinking about him, what it would be like to kiss him…

"Do you like my daddy?"

Amanda's sudden query drew Kristina out of her stupor. "Well, honey, so far I like your daddy, but we don't really know each other all that well. That's why I'm here."

Amanda nodded. "And to play with me."

She touched the tip of Amanda's upturned nose. "Yes, sweetie, and to play with you."

Amanda brought out the second case full of doll clothing and rummaged through it. "My mommy died," she said, sounding almost matter-of-fact.

Drew had told Kristina in the e-mails that he was a widower, but he'd provided no details other than that his wife had passed away years ago. "Do you remember your mommy, Mandy?"

She shrugged. "No. But Nana Lilly says I look like her."

Kristina reached out and brushed back the fringed bangs resting on Amanda's forehead. "Do you think so?"

She shrugged again. "I don't know what she looks like."

"You haven't seen any pictures?"

"Daddy doesn't have any pictures."

Kristina's chest constricted with sadness. Obviously Drew's wife's death had been so painful that he'd tucked away the reminders. But had he tucked away the memories? Was he still pining for Amanda's mother? Was that the reason for his loneliness?

Still, Amanda deserved to know such an important part of her history. Not knowing couldn't be good for a child, yet Kristina realized it wasn't her place to remind Drew of that fact. Not yet, anyway. "Maybe you should ask Daddy to see a picture, Mandy."

Amanda handed Kristina a tiny wedding dress. "It's okay. You can be my mommy now."

Kristina sighed. What had she gotten herself into? What if this didn't work out with Drew? A woman Amanda considered to be a mother figure, when she seemed to need one so badly, would once again leave her.

But it didn't have to be that way.

Despite her concerns, Kristina chose to be optimistic and hope that things would work out between her and Drew. And if they did, then perhaps she could be a mother for Amanda and a wife to Drew. If only she felt more confident that would happen.

Amanda held up the boy doll, now dressed in a miniature tuxedo. "This is Drew."

Amanda was a daddy's girl, through and through, Kristina realized. Not surprising since he was all that she had, and vice versa.

Kristina finished dressing her unrealistic curvaceous doll in a white satin bridal gown. "And what shall we call her?"

"Kristina. She's going to marry my daddy." Amanda made the declaration with certainty and a sweet smile, with optimism afforded by her youth. If only Kristina could be so sure.

Amanda took both of the dolls, held them up, and said, "I announce you man and wife," then pressed them face-to-face and made kissing noises.

"Short ceremony," Kristina said with a laugh.

"Maybe Barbie and Ken are ready for the honeymoon."

Drawn to the sound of the compelling voice, Kristina glanced toward the door to find Drew leaning against the frame wearing a navy polo shirt and white casual pants, his wavy dark hair combed neatly into place. He also wore a grin, his blue eyes sparkling with amusement. Kristina immediately responded to his presence with warmth, with wistfulness when she realized his smile was for his daughter, not for her.

"They're not Barbie and Ken, Daddy," Amanda said, sounding thoroughly put out. "It's Drew and Kristina."

Drew strolled into the room, hands in pockets. The scent of woodsy cologne caressed Kristina as he crouched beside Amanda. "I've got to go to the office for a while, so give Daddy a kiss, sweetheart." He pointed at his now clean-shaven cheek, and it took everything in Kristina not to comply, though she knew he was talking to his daughter.

Amanda frowned. "Can't you play with me and Kristina, Daddy?"

He centered his blue-flame eyes and knowing grin on Kristina. "Maybe we can play later tonight."

Kristina's pulse did double time over the double entendre. He kept staring at her, as if awaiting a response she wasn't capable of giving. From the sexy look on his face and the sensual promise in his voice, she could tell his idea of playing had nothing to do with dressing dolls. More like undressing each other. Or maybe she was simply wishing…

He finally broke their shared gaze and turned his attention to Amanda. "I'll be back after lunch."

"Okay, Daddy. But hurry." Amanda finally gave in and gave him a loud smack on his cheek.

Drew straightened and addressed Kristina again, this time with a noncommittal expression. "If you don't mind feeding her lunch, there's some sandwich fixings in the fridge. Make yourself at home."

"I will," she said, although plain Kristina Simmons from Wisconsin doubted she'd ever feel at home with the oh-so-sexy Drew Connelly.

This was the one time Drew had had no choice but to leave for the office when it wasn't completely job-related.

Blowing out a frustrated sigh, he kicked back in the chair at his desk in the seventeenth-floor office at Connelly Towers, home to the textile-manufacturing corporation his grandfather had established and his father had molded into a prestigious multi-million-dollar business. Two hours before, Kristina Simmons had given him a simple hug that had set his body to blazing. One hour before, she'd looked entirely at home in Amanda's bedroom, playing dolls with his daughter. She'd also looked entirely too sexy with her legs crossed and her skirt hiked up, inadvertently giving him a nice glimpse of tanned thigh, the reason why he'd hightailed it out of there at breakneck speed, trying hard to escape the images of running his hands up those thighs—and higher.

Thanks to that scenario, he was unable to get his mind on the recent deal he'd sealed in Europe involving a lucrative shipment of lace. The only lace he cared about at the moment was the kind that covered a woman intimately. See-through lace covering Kristina Simmons, his presumed fiancée. He needed to get that image out of his head and fast. Easier said than done.

He still couldn't believe the way she had breezed into his life that morning, turning his world upside down, turning his libido into a time bomb in a matter of minutes. Thanks to his grandmother's scheming.

Drew still had no idea how he was going to put an end to this farce, especially since his daughter seemed so taken with Kristina. He couldn't blame Mandy, but he didn't have to join her. As long as he remained objective, kept his head in the game, his hands to himself, and came up with ways to convince Kristina it would never work between them, then eventually he could go back to his life the way it was before he'd met her this morning.

And that was a life that included a few superficial women who demanded nothing more from him than an occasional escort and meaningless sex for the sake of physical gratification. No ties, no tear-filled goodbyes. Nothing complicated. Nothing that warranted any emotional commitment. Nothing but loneliness.

Now he sounded like Lilly. He didn't need anything more. He didn't need a steady relationship, a woman in his life. But Amanda did. She deserved that much. And

Kristina Simmons deserved a man who could give her a commitment. He wasn't that man, at least not at present.

For that reason, getting involved with Kristina was out of the question. Maybe someday, when the old wounds began to heal and the scars began to fade, Drew might consider settling down again. Maybe after the guilt over Talia's death subsided. Maybe when he felt that he could give a woman all of himself—if and when that ever happened.

Until then, he'd go about his business, giving Amanda his unconditional love, exactly what she gave him, despite his many flaws. He'd let this thing with Kristina play out for a month, and by that time—if not before—she would come to realize that she was better off without him.

The sound of a voice coming from the hallway dragged him back to the situation at hand. His father's voice, to be exact. "I'm telling you, something's going on with Charlotte. Tom Reynolds told me she's been acting very mysteriously, coming into the office while we've been at the lake on the weekends, avoiding people…"

Drew listened carefully, curious to find out what Tom Reynolds had said about Charlotte Masters, Drew's father's trusted assistant. The detective, along with another named Lucas Starwind, had been hired by the Connellys when Drew's oldest brother, Daniel, now ruler of the kingdom of Altaria—his mother's homeland—had been the victim of an assassination attempt. The investigation had widened, putting everyone under suspicion, including all of the Connelly clan. So far everyone in the family had been cleared, much to Drew's relief. Still, the circumstances behind the attempt on Daniel's life remained a mystery.

But Charlotte Masters a suspect? Surely not, Drew

thought. Then something dawned on him. When Drew had been outside the building with his brother Rafe not long ago, Rafe had tried to talk to Charlotte and she'd avoided him like the plague. Drew had found that odd, since Charlotte and Rafe had always enjoyed engaging in friendly and sometimes acerbic banter. But that day she'd seemed aloof, as if something was bugging her.

"Grant, dear, think about it…"

Drew's gaze snapped to the door when he recognized the feminine voice. What was his mother doing here? Must be something really serious, he decided.

"You know exactly what I mean," Emma Connelly continued. "Having a baby can make you somewhat stressed. You should realize that after living with me through seven pregnancies. I'm certain that's the case with Charlotte."

Charlotte Masters pregnant? He'd spoken to his father on numerous occasions, and he couldn't recall Grant saying a word about Charlotte's pregnancy. That didn't make any sense. But then his father had been rather distracted lately over the problems with Drew's brother, Daniel. Still, the news came as quite a shock to Drew since Charlotte wasn't involved with anyone, at least not that he knew of. But stranger things had happened.

Drew smiled when he thought about his twin brother and the rude awakening Brett was in for with a baby about to arrive in a matter of weeks. Drew couldn't imagine his one-time playboy brother changing diapers, doling out bottles. He also couldn't stop the little nip of envy over Brett's good fortune in finding a loving wife in former police investigator Elena Delgado, a woman who would no doubt be a good mother.

Funny, he and Brett had reversed roles. Drew had become a father at twenty-one because he'd been a careless kid; Brett had spent years actively playing the field with women numbering close to the national debt. Now Brett had settled down with the woman of his dreams and Drew had been unexpectedly thrust into the dating scene. He never had been, or ever would be, as good at it as Brett.

The continuing conversation outside his door caught Drew's attention once again. His mother was close to shouting, or as close as the genteel Emma could get.

"I don't care if he's working, Grant. We have to settle this with Drew now. And you're coming with me to do that."

Uh-oh, Drew thought. This couldn't be good.

The door opened to his mother, former Princess Emma Rosemere of Altaria, dressed to the nines in Dior, elegant and regal as she stepped into the office with a grace befitting her royal status before his father had whisked her away to America to become a Connelly.

"Hello, Drew," she said, nervously patting blond hair pulled up in a twist, the way she'd worn it for as long as Drew could remember.

Drew tossed his pen aside and straightened. For some reason he always came to attention in her presence like one of her royal subjects. "Hello, Mother. What brings you down to the office on a Saturday?"

She glided to the edge of his desk, her delicate features stern. "Your father and I need to speak with you."

Drew leaned to one side and looked around her, toward the open door. "Fine, but I don't see Dad."

Emma glanced over her shoulder. "Where did that man go?"

"I'm right here, Emma, so don't get your corset in a kink." His father slipped in, looking decidedly uncomfortable. He tugged at the collar on his lucky green golf shirt then slicked a hand through his black hair.

Drew figured he might as well get it over with, although he had no idea what "it" was. "So to what do I owe this pleasure, playing audience to my parents?"

Emma's eyes misted, indicating this was serious business. "I can't believe you didn't tell us."

"Tell you what?"

"That you're engaged."

Good news traveled fast in the Connelly family. So did the bad and the bizarre. "How did you find out?" As if he didn't know.

"Your grandmother told us."

Lilly, Mouth of the Midwest, strikes again.

"It came about rather suddenly." An understatement of the first order.

"Where did you meet her, son?" his father asked.

In my hallway this morning.

Nope, Drew couldn't say that. The fewer people who knew about the scheme, the better. Not to protect Lilly, but to protect Kristina. "At a singles' club." That sounded logical and a modified version of the truth.

"A singles' club?" His mother sounded exasperated and looked as though she might actually lose her composure. "What do you know about her? Is she suitable?"

Drew couldn't contain his sarcasm over the third degree. "Well, Mom, actually she's a stripper I picked up in some dive off Michigan Avenue. I tipped her good and she came home with me."

Emma paled and laid a hand on her chest beneath the string of cultured pearls. "Oh...my...goodness."

"I think he's kidding, Emma," Grant said. "If you'll recall, Lilly told us she's a kindergarten teacher."

"She is?" Drew blurted out, then cleared his throat.

"I meant, yes, she is. A very good one. Amanda loves her." That was the absolute truth.

Emma sank into the chair across from Drew's desk. "I hope you know what you're doing this time, Drew."

In other words, Drew thought, don't make the same mistakes you made with your first wife. "I know what I'm doing, Mother. I'm not some college kid caught in the throes of hormones."

Emma once again composed her features. "What is this woman's name?"

At least he knew that much. "Kristina Simmons."

"Does she live in the city?"

Obviously Lilly had left out a few important details when she'd spilled the beans. "She lives very close to me."

Emma's smile was tentative. "In your neighborhood?"

No way around the truth since his parents would eventually find out. "Not just in my neighborhood. She lives with me."

Emma's eyes went wide. "Oh, Drew, that shouldn't be going on with Amanda in the house."

Little did his mother know, *that* wasn't going on at all, at least not beyond Drew's imagination. "Don't panic, Mother. She has her own room. We decided on the living arrangement since we thought it best to get to know each other better, to make sure we're compatible before we take the plunge."

Drew felt as if he'd already taken the plunge, and he was damn near drowning in deceit.

His father moved behind Emma and rested his hands on her shoulders. "That sounds like a wise decision, Drew. We trust that you'll do right by this woman and your daughter."

"Thanks, Dad. I'll try." Little did they know that in a month's time, maybe less, it would all be over.

"We really must meet her soon," Emma said.

"You're right," Grant agreed. "And the perfect time to do that is next weekend."

Great. All Drew needed was to have to put up a front with his whole family in attendance. He had to come up with something quick. "I was planning to take Amanda and Kristina to mine and Brett's lake house for the weekend. Brett won't be needing it since Elena's not up to traveling right now because of her pregnancy, so I thought it would be a good time to show her the place."

"That's perfect," Emma said. "We'll come there, invite the family and make a weekend of it at the lake."

Did she have an answer for everything? "Mother, the place isn't big enough to house the whole family."

"It's big enough for a casual dinner. And after that's over, we can go back and spend the night at the cottage. We have plenty of room there." Emma stood. "I need to start making some calls to the children. I imagine some won't be able to come until Saturday, so we'll have a barbecue then. Friday night we'll have a small dinner with just your father and I and Lilly and Tobias..."

Drew's head began to swim, but he wouldn't even try to come up with an excuse to get out of the little soiree. His mother was on a roll, and no one could stop Princess Emma when she was on a roll.

He would just have to convince Kristina to break off the engagement before the weekend. But he had to be in Canada on Monday, returning on Thursday. That gave him next to no time to change Kristina's mind about the engagement, about him.

He'd simply have to work harder, beginning the minute he got home.

Three

Drew halted in the foyer at the sound of the bluesy voice singing an equally bluesy number. A fantastic feminine voice capable of making even the most stoic man stop to listen.

The song seemed familiar, but Drew couldn't quite recall where or when he'd heard it. A sensual song that spoke of firsts. First encounters, first kisses. First lovemaking, although that came across with symbolism. But Drew didn't have any problem interpreting the message in the veiled lyrics. If his hunches were correct, he knew who was singing, and it wasn't his daughter.

He could only continue to listen, enthralled, until reality hit home when he noted the piano accompaniment. *Talia's piano.*

Drew strode toward the adjoining room that housed the baby grand, a room he intentionally kept closed off to avoid the memories.

With each step, the anger mounted, and so did the guilt that still lived deep within Drew. He had given Talia the piano on her twentieth birthday, and that same night had taken away her dreams of playing professionally by getting her pregnant. Then came Talia's depression after Amanda was born, her inability to cope with the demands of being a mother and the end of her career, something Drew had disregarded. He'd been too involved in his studies, too caught up in his need to establish his position within the Connelly dynasty. Eventually he'd acknowledged that friends and family had been right about Talia's problems, but not before it was too late.

As he'd suspected, he found Kristina sitting at the piano, the only thing of Talia's he'd kept when he'd built this house after her death. A reminder of his failure.

Kristina's back was to the door, her long fingers whisking over the keys with precise movements. Amanda was sitting beside her.

"What's going on in here?" Drew asked lightly in an attempt to maintain some control over his temper.

Kristina stopped playing and glanced over her shoulder. Amanda did the same, a vibrant smile plastered on her face—a face much like her mother's, calling up more memories.

"Hi, Daddy," Mandy said. "Kristina sings so pretty, doesn't she?" Her tone was full of awe, and so was her expression.

"I prefer something a bit more upbeat." He preferred to leave this room.

Kristina only grinned, turned back to the keys, and immediately went into a lively rendition of "Chopsticks."

Drew tried to keep calm, to moderate his tone. "I also

prefer that Amanda not come in here. The piano is expensive, not a play toy. It belonged to my wife.''

Kristina swiveled around to face him with a remorseful expression. ''I'm afraid that's my fault. When I told Mandy I play, she told me about the piano. I asked her to show me.''

''She knows better.''

Amanda shifted around on the seat and hung her head, looking contrite. ''But, Daddy, I wasn't bothering Mommy's piano. We didn't hurt anything.''

Drew recognized that, but he couldn't seem to get a grip on his turbulent emotions. ''Go to your room, Mandy.''

''But, Daddy—''

''No buts, Amanda Elizabeth. I need to speak with Kristina.''

Kristina hugged Amanda close to her side. ''Do what your daddy says, okay? I'll see you in a bit.''

Amanda slowly scooted off the bench then turned back to Kristina. ''Will you ask him?''

''We'll see.''

Amanda brushed past Drew without looking at him. He'd been too hard on her, all because of his guilt, his anger. He'd have to apologize later. First, he had to talk to Kristina, set some ground rules.

Kristina stood, wringing her hands. ''I didn't know the piano belonged to your wife. If I had known, I wouldn't have come in here without asking you.''

''From now on, I hope that you do ask.''

''I will.'' Her features softened into sympathy. ''I imagine it's difficult facing reminders of a woman you loved, one who's no longer with you.''

She had no idea how difficult, Drew thought. He didn't want her pity, and he wasn't in the mood to discuss Talia, yet he feared that's exactly where this conversation was heading. Best to opt for a subject change. "What did Mandy want you to ask me?"

Kristina moved away from the piano but failed to look at him. "Actually, two things. First, her friend Sara called and invited her to a swim party."

"Where?"

"At the Andersons' home, two blocks away, Amanda said. It's a sleepover."

"She can go for a while, but she can't spend the night."

Kristina finally met his gaze. "Why not?"

"I'm gone too much as it is. When I'm home, I want her here with me."

"It's only one night, and she's really looking forward to it. She told me it would be her first slumber party."

"I can't let her do it."

Now Kristina looked irritated, impatient. "I know it's probably none of my business—"

"You're right, it's not." Did he have to sound like such a jerk?

"For Amanda's sake, I'm going to continue." She paused for a deep breath. "I know it's been hard on her, on you both, since her mother's death. And I know it's difficult for you to let go. But she needs to spend time with friends, not cooped up in this house with only her toys to pass the hours while you're away."

"She spends time with friends when she's at school."

"It's not the same, Drew. It's important that children socialize outside of school with their peers."

"And what makes you the expert?" Man, that was a low blow. If he kept this up, Kristina might be out the door before day's end. Exactly what he'd planned. But he didn't want her to hate him, and if he didn't calm down, she would.

"I'm a teacher, remember?" she said in an even tone, totally undaunted by his attitude. "I told you that in the e-mails."

Those damned e-mails again. "This has to do with *my* daughter and what I think is best for her."

"She needs you, Drew, but she also needs to establish some independence."

God, he knew she was right. Still, he couldn't stand the thought of turning Amanda loose in a world that was so full of disappointments, regrets, danger. "I'll think about it." For a minute, then he would gently tell his daughter no. "What's the other thing?"

"She wants me to teach her how to play the piano."

"Absolutely out of the question."

"Why?"

"She's too young." *Too much like her mother.*

Kristina's gaze didn't waver. "On the contrary, she's exactly the right age. I taught her a few notes this afternoon and she picked them up right away. She has a gift."

Exactly like her mother, Drew thought. If he consented to the lessons, he would be forcing Kristina further into his daughter's life, into his life. If he didn't, he might be denying Amanda a chance to hone that gift, exactly what he'd done to Talia. "I'll think about that, too." And he would, seriously, but not now. Not with Kristina looking at him expectantly, kindness in her eyes, not judgment, regardless of how he'd treated her.

She sent him a hesitant smile. "All I'm asking, all that Amanda's asking, is for you to give her a chance to learn."

Drew took another moment to study Kristina, an insightful, remarkable woman whose beauty radiated from the inside out. A woman who didn't back down when it came to something she believed in, and she obviously believed in Amanda.

She was nothing like Talia, and maybe that was what he found so appealing. Talia had been self-absorbed, sophisticated, young. Kristina was unselfish, untainted, wise.

Drew couldn't seem to stop the need to take her in his arms, hold her, thank her for considering his daughter's well-being. But he did stop it, with a lot of effort.

His earlier reaction when he'd discovered Kristina at the piano only served to remind him that he had too much emotional baggage for a woman as inherently good as Kristina Simmons to handle. She didn't deserve his problems, his inability to commit. He didn't deserve someone like her.

On that thought, he turned away. He had to leave Kristina before he did something really inadvisable, like kiss her from gratitude, from a desire that didn't make any sense. He couldn't do that and still maintain his emotional bearings.

"Where are you going?" she called after him in that raspy voice of hers, the one responsible for the sudden spear of heat launching through him.

"I'm going to apologize to Amanda."

And after that, he planned to retire to his study and try to retrieve those blasted e-mails. While he was at it, he might as well make a list of demands. Contrived demands he would present to Kristina that would make her think twice about getting seriously involved with him. Maybe then she would get out of his life, if not out of his head.

* * *

"What are you doing?"

Kristina pivoted from the stove and met Drew's steady gaze. She turned down the heat under the burner, but the room was still very warm, thanks to Drew's presence.

Leaning back against the counter, she said, "I thought I'd make some dinner for us. I assumed you'd probably be too tired to go out."

He rubbed a hand over his nape and stared at the floor. "I hope you aren't making too much. Amanda will be eating at the party."

Some of the weight lifted from Kristina's heart. Father and daughter had apparently made amends this afternoon. "Then you're going to let her go?"

"Yeah. And she talked me into letting her spend the night. She has a knack for doing that kind of thing."

Kristina couldn't hold back the smile. "She'll have a wonderful time, Drew."

"I guess so," he said, followed by a long sigh.

"She'll be fine. Remember, it's just a slumber party, not her first date."

Drew groaned. "Did you have to remind me of that?"

"Sorry, but life goes on whether we want it to or not. Children grow up."

"Too fast." Drew strolled to the stove and lifted the lid on the pan. "What are you making?"

"German potato salad."

He raised an eyebrow after closing the lid. "German, huh?"

"Yes, my grandmother's recipe. I come from good German stock on my father's side." And inherited a solid German build from her father's mother, although Kristina could swear there was some Amazon thrown in somewhere.

"Do you see your family often?" Drew asked.

Kristina shook her head. "Not in a while. My father

passed away a few years back. My mother and I don't talk that often.''

Drew frowned. "Problems?''

"No, not really. She's very busy taking care of my sister Carina's two children." Dear Carina, whose body naturally repelled fat.

"I can't imagine not staying in touch with your family.''

No, he probably couldn't, Kristina thought, considering how close he was to his own family. But he probably hadn't endured constant criticism of things he had no power over, like his natural build. Kristina had. Her mother had meant well, and she hadn't been exactly cruel, but their conversations had always been the same.

Kristina, honey, are you watching your weight? Kristina, I found a new diet you might want to try. Kristina, how do you expect to find a boyfriend unless you take care of yourself?

In other words, how would Kristina ever get a man unless she starved herself?

Kristina had tried to diet in the past, but she wasn't genetically inclined to be small, so she had finally resigned herself to the fact that she would simply have to learn to live with her body type. Unfortunately, her mother never had.

Kristina stirred the potatoes with a vengeance, with the force of resurrected resentment. "I still call her now and then when I have the opportunity.''

"Feel free to call while you're here," Drew said, then added, "Sunday would be best. Cheaper rates.''

Cheaper rates? Odd, Kristina thought, considering Drew was anything but destitute. "Okay. Thank you.''

Drew surveyed the stove again. "What else are we having?''

At the moment, Kristina was having a strong urge to hug him since he looked so great. "I found a couple of steaks in the freezer. I have them ready for the broiler."

"I want mine medium rare."

"So do I, so that's not a problem."

Something else they had in common. This was going better than she'd expected, with the exception of the piano incident. She certainly understood his reticence in that respect. From now on she would tread lightly when it came to his personal space, at least until they knew each other better.

He leaned a hip against the counter and faced her. "I'm surprised you found anything to prepare. My housekeeper only comes in two days a week and she has her hands full with her regular duties, so I haven't restocked in a while. And Amanda's nanny wasn't much of a shopper beyond frozen dinners and pizza."

"I can do some shopping tomorrow afternoon. I'll take Amanda with me."

He shrugged. "Fine by me. She'll probably enjoy that."

"Which reminds me," Kristina said. "Your grandfather told me you're without a nanny at the moment."

"Yeah. I'll contact the agency first thing Monday morning. Meanwhile, my grandmother will keep an eye on Mandy."

"Is that really necessary since I'm here?"

His smile appeared, only halfway, but at least it was a smile. "I don't know. Is it?"

"I don't mind looking after Amanda, at least until school starts. And even then, I'll be off work in time to pick her up."

"Work?"

"Yes. My new job at the Montessori school about twenty minutes from here. Remember?"

He hesitated as if carefully choosing his response, then stated sternly, "I prefer my wife not work outside the home."

"But that's not what you said in the—"

"E-mail, I know. I changed my mind."

"Just like that?"

"Yeah. Is there a problem?"

Oh, yes. A big problem. "I love my job, Drew." She loved being with children who didn't pass judgment on her because of her size. "I'm not one to sit at home doing nothing."

"Believe me, you'll have plenty to do."

"Such as?"

He inched a little closer. "Laundry. I like my shirts ironed with nice creases."

"What, no cleaners around here?"

"Yes, but they don't do them the way I like. I'm very particular."

Obviously he'd never heard of permanent press. But gosh, he smelled great, looked gorgeous. That alone was worth ironing a dozen or so shirts, at least until she could find a suitable dry cleaner. "No problem. I like to iron. Getting those creases just right makes me feel like I've really accomplished something." She couldn't contain her sarcasm.

"And the house. It's big. Lots of upkeep."

"I thought you said you have a housekeeper."

He paused as if considering that for a moment. "Yeah, right now. But I'll probably fire her after our wedding. Save a little money."

From the looks of the house, she assumed he probably had a fortune to spare. Funny, she wouldn't have pegged

Drew as a penny-pincher, but that frugality could explain his obvious wealth. Not a bad trait, Kristina decided, since she'd been brought up to be conservative in her spending. "Shall I do the lawn, too?" she teased.

"No, I have a service. You wouldn't have enough time to do the lawn. But then again—" he rubbed a hand over his jaw "—you maybe could work that in. I'll have to think on it."

Was this some kind of a joke? A test? Kristina couldn't tell from the noncommittal expression on Drew's face. She suspected he wasn't serious, so she'd play along for now. "I can handle a mower. I used to shred pasture to earn extra money when I was in high school."

He suddenly looked thoughtful, as if really considering having her mow and prune. "The lawn's not that big, so you could probably handle it. And we can't forget my social life. Lots of parties. The Connellys love to give parties."

Oh, joy. "I suppose that means we'll be entertaining."

"Of course."

"Anything else?" As if that wasn't enough.

"Yeah. The most important thing."

Hopefully this didn't entail working on his car, although, thanks to her dad, the mechanic, she'd learned to change oil and tires. Not that she dared mention that to Drew. "What important thing?"

He slid closer until she could count every dark lash framing his crystal-blue eyes, every whisker blanketing his evening-shadowed jaw. "Kids. Lots of 'em. My mother had eight, so I think that's a good number to start with."

To start with? "You didn't mention that to me."

"I didn't say anything in the e-mail because I didn't want to scare you off."

He was doing a pretty darned good job of it now. But Kristina refused to be that easily intimidated. After all, the process of making babies with Drew wasn't an unpleasant prospect. Not in the least. Still, she hoped to convince him that moderation might be favorable to having a litter, if this worked out between them.

She patted her hips and watched his eyes follow the movement. "That's why I have these. I'm sure I'll have no trouble accommodating lots of babies."

And I hope you'll be able to take off the excess weight when the time comes, Kristina. Darn her mother.

"Then, eight kids it is," Drew said with a victorious smile.

Kristina had the sneaking suspicion that she might have gravely misjudged Drew Connelly, and not in a good way. But she firmly believed that people had the capacity for change, and that included Slave Driver Drew. At least he hadn't mentioned putting her on a diet. That would have had her heading out the door in record time.

"So let me get this straight," she said. "If we decide to get married, I'm to do all the household chores, entertain, have at least eight babies *and* do the lawn?"

His smile cracked wide open. "Okay, you can forget about the lawn."

She laid a dramatic hand across her chest, relieved to realize that he probably was teasing her. "I am so glad. I don't think that would be a very pretty sight, me pushing a lawn mower barefoot and pregnant."

"It's a riding mower." He reached out and stroked his knuckles down her cheek. "I'd want to get started right away."

"On the lawn?"

"On getting you pregnant."

Her breath hitched hard in her chest. "You don't mean tonight, do you?"

His grin was wicked and incredibly sexy. "Now, that's a thought."

A long silence passed between them as he cupped her cheek and rubbed one calloused thumb back and forth over her jaw. He inclined his head and surveyed her face, centering his gaze on her lips. Then slowly, slowly, he lowered his head....

"Daddy! Kristina!"

They both stepped back and turned simultaneously toward the kitchen entrance just as Amanda came running in, a little purple suitcase clutched in her hand.

Thank heavens for the interruption, Kristina thought. Otherwise she might have found herself in the middle of conception in the kitchen. Not a good thing for a six-year-old to witness, not to mention she wasn't ready for that to happen yet, no matter how persuasive Drew could be. Not until she knew for a fact that he did care for her. That there really could be a future for them both. That he wasn't really serious in his demands.

"Are you ready, big girl?" Kristina asked with a grin that matched Amanda's.

She nodded her head with a jerk. "Yes, ma'am."

"Did you pack your toothbrush?"

Amanda patted the case. "In here. And my pajamas and two shirts and some jeans and my bear, Bubba."

Drew ruffled Amanda's hair. "Sounds like you're ready, sweetheart, so let's get going or we'll be late."

"Dinner should be ready by the time you get back," Kristina told Drew.

He checked the clock on the oven. "Good. I like to eat at six-thirty on the dot."

Kristina might have saluted had Amanda not held out her arms and said, "Goodbye kiss, Kristina."

Kristina crouched down, kissed the little girl's cheek and accepted one in return. "Have fun, okay?"

Amanda pulled back, her eyes shining with excitement. "I will. You make sure Daddy isn't lonely, okay?"

Oh, heavens. "I'll see what I can do."

"Where's my kiss?"

Kristina glanced up to see Drew holding out his arms to his daughter. Amanda pointed to her lips. "Right on the smacker, Big Daddy."

Drew pulled Amanda up into his strong arms and sent noisy kisses all over her face until he had her giggling without mercy. Kristina looked on, thinking there was something inherently good about a man who loved his daughter so very much, even a demanding man.

Sliding her back to her feet, Drew took Amanda's hand. "Is that enough kisses for now, sweetheart?"

"Uh-huh. You have to save some for later."

"You bet."

Amanda looked at Drew, then at Kristina, then back at Drew. "You have to save some kisses for Kristina, too, Daddy."

Kristina's pulse skittered when Drew pinned her in place with eyes that darkened to a deep blue. "You're right, Mandy. I'll have to save some kisses for Kristina."

Four

"Well, darn."

Drew wondered what had Kristina suddenly so discouraged, since he hadn't been able to discourage her in the least. At dinner she'd been as cordial as ever and had kept the topic focused on Amanda, not once mentioning his list of demands. Not that he'd meant any of them. He hadn't meant to almost kiss her, either. He'd really wanted to, though. He still did. But he wouldn't. Not yet.

"What's wrong?" he asked as he joined her on the sofa and slid his mug of coffee onto the table before them.

She folded the newspaper in neat creases and tossed it next to his cup. "Wrestling's not on tonight. They're showing some kind of documentary on the history of beer. I guess we'll have to find something else to do."

Drew could think of several things to do with Kristina,

including a few of his own wrestling moves, but he figured none would be considered acceptable to her.

"We could watch a movie," he offered. A cartoon, he decided, because if he brought out a film that was the least bit suggestive, he might make good on his conception suggestion. Not that he wanted more kids. Mandy was all he would ever need. Still, he wouldn't mind rehearsing with Kristina, and he had to get that out of his head immediately before he took her down for the count on the sofa.

At the moment, Kristina wasn't helping his predicament at all. She'd changed into an oversize pale yellow T-shirt and black leggings, a relatively innocuous outfit, but Drew wasn't feeling the least bit innocent tonight.

She faced him and tucked one leg beneath her, her arm draped over the back of the couch. "You know, we could forgo the TV altogether and talk."

Talk? The woman was amazing. After what he'd said to her earlier, he was surprised she was speaking to him at all. But nothing he'd done or said to this point had seemed to faze her. Neither did the fact that the T-shirt she wore slipped off her shoulders, giving Drew a nice glimpse of tanned bare skin. He sure as hell couldn't claim that wasn't affecting him. And right now he wasn't sure he could carry on a decent conversation when he was having some pretty indecent thoughts. But he'd better try.

"What do you want to talk about?" he asked, fighting the urge to let his gaze linger on her breasts outlined by the thin fabric.

She gave him a bare-shouldered shrug. "Things we didn't cover in the e-mails, I guess."

He'd definitely have to guess about that, especially after discovering Lilly had learned a lot during his absence, including how to use the delete button. He hadn't found even one of the e-mails, so again he was jumping into rough waters, totally blind. "What haven't we covered?"

She tilted her head, one dark brow raised in a question mark. "What were you like in high school?"

"Very serious."

"About what?"

"What do you mean?"

"School? Sports?" She grinned. "Girls?"

He returned her smile with a cynical one. "My brother Brett was good with the girls, not me."

"Not one girlfriend?"

"Oh, I had a few, but most of them eventually decided they liked Brett better."

Kristina released a raspy laugh that had Drew coming to full attention. Every bit of him. "How could they tell the difference since you're identical twins?"

Obviously Lilly hadn't left out that detail. "Brett was more charming, a big talker. I was more interested in being a good student." Until his family had introduced him to Talia. Then he'd discovered just how much he appreciated girls, eventually to his own detriment.

"I did play baseball," he added.

Kristina's brown eyes widened. "What position?"

"Pitcher."

"Really? I was a catcher on the softball team."

"Tough position."

"Well, let's just say these came in handy," she said, patting her thighs.

Drew realized that Kristina was well versed at using self-deprecating humor to cover her discomfort over her size. If she only knew that the image of her thighs cradling his thighs was foremost on his mind, and it wasn't at all objectionable. In fact, it was downright exciting to think about.

He cleared his throat and cleared the fantasy out of his mind, at least for the time being. He'd put her through enough mental calisthenics today. But what he had in mind had everything to do with a physical workout.

On that thought, he turned the conversation to a safe, general topic. "So you played sports, huh?"

She toyed with the hem of her shirt with long fingers, sparking Drew's randy imagination back to life. "Absolutely. Volleyball, basketball. My height served me well in that regard."

He figured she could probably serve him well, too, and he didn't mean by ironing his shirts or mowing the lawn. "I know a lot of women who'd like to have your height."

She rolled her eyes. "Yeah, well, obviously they haven't experienced being taller than most of the boys in school."

Drew inched a little closer as if his body had developed a brain. He was pretty sure one part had, because right now it was speaking to him, loud and clear. "You didn't find one boy that was taller?"

Her gaze faltered. "Oh, there were a few, but none that were interested. Not until college." Her tone was laced with regret, and Drew wanted to know why.

"A serious relationship, I take it," he said.

"I thought it had potential since he seemed very attentive in the beginning. Great looking and charming. A sweet-talker. That should have been my first clue that he wasn't being totally honest."

A twinge of guilt rose up in Drew. Little did Kristina know he wasn't so hot in the honesty department, either. "What happened?"

She threaded her bottom lip between her teeth. "I accompanied him to a party at his fraternity house where he nominated me for one of their esteemed awards.''

"Award?''

"Yes. The Mount Vesuvius Award, given to the largest girl at the party. I discovered that he'd basically taken me out to set me up for that sterling moment.''

Drew shook his head, experiencing a gut-level anger. "I'm sorry, Kristina. Those damn frat houses are full of creeps. You're better off without him.''

"Don't be sorry.'' She shifted slightly, indicating her unease. "I survived, and as a plus, I came away much wiser for having gone through the experience.''

Drew admired her wisdom, her honesty, and hated like hell that she'd been the target of some jerk. She didn't deserve that kind of treatment. More and more, he was beginning to realize that fact. Which left him in a quandary. How was he supposed to call off the engagement without totally ripping out her heart in the process? What would she think if she knew that he was deceiving her even though he was doing so to protect her feelings?

He needed more time to think, a difficult prospect with her sitting there looking way too sexy to ignore.

"No other lovers?'' he asked. He wasn't sure why that would matter, but it did.

She frowned. "Who said he was my lover?''

"He wasn't?''

"No. I haven't had one.''

Oh, hell. "You're saying you haven't—''

"Made love with anyone?'' She looked away. "No, I haven't. I've always believed that a solid commitment should exist before a person takes that all-important step. Up to this point in my life, that hasn't happened.''

Kristina was a virgin, something that probably shouldn't surprise Drew, considering her conviction.

Talia had been inexperienced when he'd made love to her that first time, but she had been barely nineteen. For all intents and purposes, with the exception of one fumbled encounter with a willing woman his senior year of high school, Drew hadn't been all that experienced either. In recent years, he'd tried to play catch-up, but not in a while. Certainly not with any woman that even remotely resembled Kristina, inside or out.

Kristina was strong in her beliefs that sex for the sake of having sex was out of the question. This might be his answer. He could go back to plan A, modified somewhat, and try to use his powers of persuasion. But he had to be careful. He wouldn't force himself on any woman. Never had, never would. That didn't mean he couldn't turn on the charm and see where it led. If Kristina decided he was moving too fast, then maybe she'd change her mind about seeing this whole thing through.

Drew took her hand into his and rubbed his fingertips over her knuckles. "I suppose this means you would want to wait until we're married before we make love."

She drew in a quick breath. "I'm not saying that. I believe that sexual compatibility is important in a relationship."

He gave her his best suggestive grin. "You mean test-drive the car before you buy it?"

A slight smile tipped the corner of her lips. "In a manner of speaking."

He draped his free arm over the back of the sofa and moved closer. "Care to go for a ride?" Man, that was one sorry line. He wouldn't be at all surprised if she slapped him, or threw him into a half nelson in honor of her favorite sport.

Instead, her grin expanded, taking Drew by storm. "I

don't think we're ready to try out the equipment just yet. Not until we find out if we're compatible in other ways."

Damn. Wasn't there anything he could propose that might ruffle her? "Then a kiss is out of the question?"

"On the first date?"

"First date?"

"This is our first date, right?"

His gaze roamed over her beautiful face, coming to rest on her tempting mouth. "Not if you consider all our e-mail dates." He wrapped his arm around her shoulder and gave her a little tug toward him, expecting her to issue a protest. She didn't.

She did lay her palm on his jean-covered thigh, a dangerous place for her hand to be considering what was happening a few inches above. Then in that to-die-for voice, she said, "Since you put it that way, I guess one kiss wouldn't hurt. After all, you did promise Amanda, didn't you?"

Drew's mind suddenly went as blank as a TV with no cable connection. *He* was the one who was supposed to be in command of this plan. *He* was the one who was supposed to shake her resolve, when in fact his control was starting to flounder. *He* was the one who should proceed with caution.

Caution left the premises the moment her eyes closed, the moment she leaned forward, bringing with her the scent of jasmine and the promise of a kiss that Drew hadn't expected her to give so easily. Still, he couldn't resist, so he headed down the path of discovery by whisking his lips over hers.

Her mouth parted beneath his, allowing him the opportunity to explore the inviting warmth. She tasted sweet, tasted like the lemon sherbet they'd had after dinner. Tasted like heaven on earth when she tentatively touched her tongue to his, sending his body on a spin straight into oblivion. He couldn't stop now even if he wanted to, and he really, really didn't want to.

The kiss intensified and so did Drew's desire when her arms moved to his shoulders and her breasts pressed against his chest. He landed his palm on the curve of her hip, and somehow she started leaning back, taking him down until he was lying on top of her. When she moved her hips, pressing against his groin, three thoughts came to mind. He was hard as granite, Kristina had forgotten her conviction and he'd totally forgotten his goal of discouraging her.

Right now she was encouraging him to be more daring, or at least that was what he presumed when a small, desperate sound escaped her lips. Unable to rationalize the reasons to stop, Drew brushed kisses down the column of her throat, then lower to her shoulder where he pushed the shirt farther down her arms. A little more and he'd have it exactly where he wanted it—completely off.

The shrill ring jerked Drew back into reality and he bolted from the sofa. The sound of Kristina's ragged breathing echoed behind him as he made his way across the room to the annoying phone. He should be grateful for the interruption. Grateful that things hadn't gone any further. Instead, he was really ticked off.

"Yeah?"

"Daddy?"

He softened his tone at the sound of his daughter's voice. "Is something wrong, Mandy?"

"I wanna talk to Kristina."

"Why?"

"C'mon, Daddy. I need to talk to Kristina. Please?"

No use trying to argue once she got something in her head. "Okay. Just a minute."

He turned to Kristina, who was watching him with guarded interest, her face flushed from his kiss and the shirt riding low at her breasts. She looked sexy as hell, and if this were anyone but his daughter on the phone, he'd hang up and continue what they'd started, even against better judgment. Finally she pulled the shirt back up and hugged her arms close to her chest, aiding him somewhat in his return to sanity.

He tipped the phone toward her. "It's Mandy. She wants to talk to you."

Kristina looked as confused as Drew felt. "Me?"

"That's what she says."

Slowly she rose and took the phone from him, strolling toward the opposite end of the room, away from him. "Hi, Mandy. What's up?"

A long silence passed until Kristina said, "Calm down, honey. It's going to be okay. Sara's your friend, right?"

Concerned, Drew stepped closer to Kristina, hoping to discover what kind of crisis his daughter was enduring. He should've made her come home after the party. She was in trouble, and she needed him. Actually, she needed Kristina, a thought that gave him pause and made him hurt a little.

"Listen to me, Mandy," Kristina said. "I want you to go and find Sara and stick with her. Does she have a stuffed animal?" More silence. "Well, see? She understands why you need your bear with you. That doesn't make you a baby."

Drew's temper soared to dangerous heights. "Someone called her a baby?"

Kristina put up a hand to silence him. "That's okay, sweetie. These things happen. Some kids make fun of other kids in order to make themselves feel better. You just have to ignore her and find your real friends. Okay?"

"I'm going to go get her," Drew said, experiencing an irrational need to rescue his daughter from the clutches of a spiteful six-year-old bully.

Kristina turned her back, blatantly ignoring him. "I promise I'll tell Daddy. Have fun and we'll see you in the morning." Another pause. "I love you, too, sweetie."

With that, Kristina clicked the phone off at the same time as Drew's heart took a nosedive. A bond between Kristina and his daughter had already been forged. A strong bond that he would be responsible for breaking. He hated even thinking about that now.

Kristina walked across the room and replaced the receiver on the cradle, then faced Drew again. "She wanted me to tell you that she's a big girl, and she loves you."

A moment passed before Drew could speak. He was torn between anger and remorse. Anger at Kristina for handling his daughter so well. Remorse because it was all too apparent how much Mandy needed a mother. How much she already needed Kristina. Yet no matter how easy needing Kristina might be, Drew couldn't allow that to happen.

He rubbed a hand over his jaw and sighed. "I should go get her. I don't like the thought of other kids making fun of her."

Kristina took a few hesitant steps forward. "It's a fact of life, Drew. I learned those lessons early on. Kids can be cruel and Mandy needs to realize that."

"She's still a baby, dammit."

"She's strong, like her daddy."

She might be strong, but she hadn't come by it honestly. Talia had been weak, frail in body and soul. Drew was still dealing with his own weaknesses, his guilt because he hadn't been strong for Talia when she'd needed him to be.

But Kristina was strong. And sensual, something he'd recently discovered when she'd been in his arms. He instinctively knew that her natural sensuality was untapped, waiting to be uncovered in the care of the right man. But he wasn't sure he deserved to be that man. He also wasn't sure he could stop himself from trying to find out.

For that reason, he turned away from her and said, "I'm going up to bed. I still have jet lag."

"Drew?"

Her tempting voice pulled him back around. "Yeah?"

"I'm sorry. I probably should've let you handle it since she's your daughter."

"You handled it fine." Better than he ever could have.

"Are you angry with me?"

More angry with himself. Angry at Lilly. Angry that he would inevitably hurt Kristina once she discovered the truth about the engagement. The truth about him. "I'm just tired."

"Are you sure?"

"I'm sure."

A lie. He was only sure about one thing. If she came any closer, he'd kiss her again, maybe even do more than that. She deserved better, and he needed to remember that. He also needed to find the strength to tell her the truth. Maybe while he was away next week, he could think of some way to do that, before he did something stupid, like make love to her knowing that he couldn't offer her more.

On Monday morning, Kristina waited downstairs to see Drew off before he left for his business trip. Amanda was still sleeping, understandable considering her busy weekend. After returning from the sleepover, she'd insisted Kristina take her to the park then grocery shopping while

Drew returned to the office for the better part of the day to prepare for his trip, or so he'd said. Kristina couldn't help but feel that he'd intentionally avoided her, and he was probably justified in doing so. Not only had she stepped over the parental bounds by intervening when Amanda had called, but she'd totally forgotten herself in Drew's arms.

Drew probably thought her to be the consummate hypocrite, in one moment stressing the importance of waiting for a commitment before lovemaking, then practically throwing herself at him on the sofa like some wild, wanton woman.

Her first clue had come last night when he'd tucked Amanda into bed early then retired without any conversation. No kiss good-night. Nothing but detachment, and she'd hated it.

Propping her elbows on the dinette table and resting her face in her hands, Kristina attempted to think of some way to let him know that she was committed to Amanda and bent on seeing this whole thing through until the time came when they reached a decision.

"Tired?"

She looked up to find Drew leaning back against the kitchen island, dressed in an immaculate navy suit, his hair impeccably groomed, his face clean-shaven. The scent of cologne overrode the smell of brewing coffee. And here Kristina sat in her worn cotton robe, her hair pulled up in a lopsided ponytail and her feet bare. At least she'd showered.

She sat back and rimmed a fingertip over her coffee cup. "I didn't get much sleep last night." Or the night before, thanks to some fairly vivid fantasies about this man.

"I know what you mean," he said while pouring his coffee.

She pushed back the chair and stood. "Would you like some breakfast?"

He checked his watch. "I don't have time. My flight leaves in less than two hours. I've got to get to the airport as soon as the driver arrives."

She focused on the centerpiece holding multicolored ceramic fruit, avoiding his eyes. "Okay."

"Kristina."

She met his solemn gaze. "Yes?"

He gripped the mug so tightly Kristina feared it might break. "I have a few things I need to tell you."

Exactly what he'd said to her when she'd shown up at his door two days ago. "I'm listening." *And worrying*.

He walked to the refrigerator and pointed to a list tacked under a happy-face magnet. "These are my parents' phone numbers in case of an emergency. The hotel where I'll be staying is up there, too. I'll call tonight and give you the room number."

Kristina folded her arms across her chest and nodded.

"And one more thing you should know," he said, sounding all too serious.

Kristina braced for the news that he'd changed his mind, that he expected her to move out once he returned home. Instead, he added, "There are two numbers at the bottom of the list. Detectives Lucas Starwind and Tom Reynolds. If you have any kind of trouble at all, call them. They're under private hire by my family."

She felt a nagging fear over needing protection mixed with relief that he hadn't called everything off. "What kind of trouble?"

"Strange phone messages. Suspicious vehicles nearby. I also have my own security posted outside at all times."

"Is Amanda in danger?"

"This doesn't have to do with Amanda, although I did

send a patrol over to the Andersons' last night just in case. This has to do with my brother Daniel.''

"The one who's ruling some kind of kingdom?"

Drew's expression reflected confusion. "How did you know about that?"

"You told me in the e-mails, but you didn't mention any kind of threat."

"I didn't want to worry you." He rubbed a hand over his neck. "Chances are, this problem with Daniel won't affect us, but we can't be too careful. Considering my family's status, anything's possible. I'd rather err on the side of caution."

"I understand." And she did to a point. Still, she couldn't help but be concerned.

The doorbell rang, spurring Drew into action. He walked into the hallway with Kristina following behind him. She wished he didn't have to go. Wished she had made him talk to her last night. But she hadn't, and it would have to wait until he returned.

Opening the door, Drew handed his bags to a man in a dark suit who turned and headed to the black limousine parked at the curb. Awareness of the Connelly's importance and wealth, namely Drew's importance, was beginning to hit home for Kristina.

Drew turned and closed the door, sheltering them from the driver's eyes, taking Kristina totally by surprise.

"I'll be back on Thursday, but it won't be until later," he said. "I'll stop by the office first."

Kristina tried to smile, but it felt artificial. "Guess I'll see you then."

His smile came halfway. "Make sure Mandy doesn't give you too much grief."

"She'll be fine. And one other thing."

"What's that?"

"Do you mind if I give her a few piano lessons? I won't do it if you don't—"

"That's fine. I'm sure she'll enjoy it."

Kristina smiled in earnest now. "We'll both enjoy it."

Drew studied her a long moment, his gaze lingering on her eyes then tracking to her mouth. She found herself hoping, just one more time before he left…

He brushed his lips over her cheek. "Take care. I'll talk to you tonight."

Not exactly what she'd had in mind, but she guessed it was better than nothing.

Drew turned toward the door, his hand braced on the knob. He hesitated, then turned back to her and, before she could prepare, took her in his arms and kissed her but good.

A deep, delving kiss. A meeting of lips and tongues and labored breaths. He held her close, made her want, made her desire to know how it would feel to let him lead her to the ultimate destination—lovemaking.

He abruptly ended the kiss then rushed away without so much as a goodbye. Kristina stared at the door long after it closed, totally enthralled, utterly confused and very close to falling completely for Drew Connelly, a man she was only beginning to understand.

Five

Drew had endured three days' worth of business meetings, going through the motions with one thought on his mind—Kristina Simmons.

They had spoken every night by phone, conversations consisting of Mandy's activities and small talk. One thing he had learned, Kristina Simmons had a wicked sense of humor. Many times they'd laughed together, yet Drew had sensed an underlying tension in what hadn't been said.

He couldn't count the times he'd almost told her how badly he'd missed her, how she had filled his dreams along with his waking hours. But he hadn't bothered to tell her any of that, or the truth behind their meeting.

Now seated on the edge of the hotel bed wearing only a towel slung low on his hips, the remnants of his barely touched dinner on the table in the next room, he was still thinking about her, wanting her when he knew he shouldn't.

So much for his plans to concoct some scheme to send her on her way. He was more uncertain now about what he wanted to do, though he knew soul deep what he needed to do. He needed to tell her everything and suffer the consequences of his deceit like a man.

He grabbed up the phone and pounded out his home number before he lost his nerve. Mandy picked up on the second ring.

"Hi, sweetheart. I thought I told you to let Kristina answer the phone."

"I know, Daddy. She's in the shower."

That was all he needed, to picture Kristina naked while talking to his daughter. Not that he hadn't thought about that a few minutes before when he was taking his own shower. "Can you have her call me?"

"Wait a minute, 'kay, Daddy?"

"Okay."

The phone pounding the floor blasted his ear, but fortunately not badly enough to render him deaf. He heard the shuffle of feet followed by Kristina's mellow voice.

The phone clanked again. "She's out now, Daddy, and she said hang on."

He was hanging on, barely. "Are you being a good girl?"

"Uh-huh. Kristina taught me some piano and she read me *Little House on the Prairie*. Debbie wouldn't read that to me."

"Sorry about that, sweetheart, but at least now you have Kristina." For the time being. "You haven't been on the computer, have you?"

"For a little while, but Kristina was with me. We went one place and learned how they make syrup."

A definite switch from the last time Mandy had encountered the Internet with his grandmother, learning how to find a husband. And finding Kristina.

"Nana Lilly called today."

Speak of the little devil herself. "What did she want?"

"To talk to Kristina."

Great. "About what?"

"I dunno. You told me not to listen when people are on the phone."

For once he'd wished Amanda had disobeyed his orders. He could only guess at what Lilly had told Kristina, but at the moment he didn't even want to try.

"Here's Kristina, Daddy."

"Okay, sweetheart. Go to bed. It's late. I love you, kiddo."

"Love you, too, Daddy."

"Hi, Drew. Wait just a sec." Kristina gave the directive to his daughter to go on up to bed, then came another exchange of "I love yous," followed by the sound of an exaggerated kiss and a few giggles.

"Okay, I'm back." She sounded winded, but then so was Drew over hearing her voice.

He cleared the hitch from his throat. "How's it going?"

"Fine, except for one thing."

"What's that?"

"Tara stopped by today looking for you."

Drew felt badly that he hadn't spoken to his sister in a while. He held a certain affinity with Tara since she, too, had lost her spouse through death, leaving her with a small son to raise on her own. "Did she need something in particular?"

"She's received some strange phone calls and thinks someone may be following her."

Drew stifled an oath. Now that Tara was finally involved with someone, she certainly didn't need anything that might interfere with her hard-earned happiness. Come to think of it, she didn't seem all that happy with John Parker. But the guy could offer Tara and her son some much-needed stability. However, Drew wasn't sure what John Parker could offer in regard to Tara's safety since he wasn't exactly the superhero type. "Is Tara okay otherwise?"

"Nervous, but as well as can be expected. She thinks she might be imagining things because of the attempt on Daniel's life, but I gave her the detectives' numbers and told her to call them, just to be on the safe side."

"Good advice." Something suddenly occurred to Drew. "She doesn't think anyone followed her to the house, does she?"

"I asked her that, but she said she didn't think so. Besides, your guards are staying very close by. I'm not worried about us, but I am concerned about her."

Drew was concerned about all of them. He couldn't stand the thought of anyone hurting his family, least of all Amanda, or Kristina. "Thanks for handling it, even if it is nothing."

Drew hesitated a moment, worried that Tara might have revealed details about Talia's death, something Drew didn't want Kristina hearing from anyone but him, if he decided to dredge that up. "So what did you two talk about?" he asked.

"Nothing much since she had to get back to her son. She did tell me that she's heard a lot of good things about me, and hoped that we would have more time to spend together later. Your grandmother said the same."

He wondered what else Lilly had said. Might as well

ask since the opportunity had presented itself. "I hope Grandmother didn't embarrass you."

"Not at all. She was very kind. Basically she wanted to welcome me to the family. She also told me that she looked forward to meeting me this weekend. Do you know what that's about?"

He'd totally forgotten about the little lake reunion. "I've been meaning to tell you about that. I have a cabin on Lake Geneva not too far from the family house. Brett and I built it a few years back. I planned to take you and Mandy there for the weekend."

"Oh, Drew, that sounds wonderful. I've been to Lake Geneva, but it was ages ago. It's a beautiful place. I can't wait."

Drew suddenly decided he couldn't lower the boom over the phone about the e-mails. That would be cowardly, to say the least. He'd have to do it after the weekend, when he had her face-to-face. Another few days shouldn't matter.

"Just so you're prepared, my family will be there," he said.

"All of them?"

Man, he hoped not. "Not likely, but I'm not sure how many since my mother is making the arrangements. I do know Brett won't be there. Since he and his wife, Elena, are about to have their first baby in a few weeks, they've decided to stick close to home."

"That's right. You told me that."

In the e-mails, he assumed.

"Anyway, I'm sure you'll fit in just fine." In fact, he'd take that to the bank. He imagined his whole family would welcome Kristina with open arms once they got to know her. She was every mother's dream, the ideal mate, the perfect prospect to be Mandy's mother. What wasn't to like? Drew couldn't think of one thing.

"Drew, I have to ask you something." She sounded way too serious, and Drew pretty much knew what would come next.

"Ask away."

"What's going on with us?"

"What do you mean?" He knew exactly what she meant.

"Well, you barely spoke to me the day before you left, but for the past few days you've been very attentive. And that morning, at the door, you…"

"Kissed you?"

"Yes. You kissed me." Her voice had a breathy quality about it. Soft, sexy, seriously seductive. His entire body came to life, every nerve and muscle. Every component, especially the one below the towel.

"I'm getting mixed signals," she continued, "and I'd like to know where I stand."

"Honestly?" he asked, wondering if maybe he should tell her what he should've told her days ago, before things had gone so far. Before he'd kissed her, held her, touched her.

"I think the truth works best," she said.

What was the truth exactly? That he wanted her out of his life, or that he wanted her with everything in him? Right now, he could only consider one truth.

"The truth is that I can't keep my hands off you. I avoided you on Sunday because I knew that if I got too close to you, I'd wind up kissing you again, maybe even carrying you to my bed."

"That would have been a feat," she teased.

"I'm serious, Kristina. I didn't want to do that with my daughter in the house."

"Oh, I see."

"I don't think you do see." Yanking the towel away, he slipped under the sheets and rested his free hand on his belly, imagining Kristina's hand there and lower.

"All I've been able to think about is you," he admitted, shocked at how easily the words left his mouth. "I enjoy talking to you. I look forward to our phone calls. I look forward to being with you again. Kissing you again. Holding you in every way."

Her breath caught. "Really?"

"But I know how you feel about making love before we're ready, and I respect that. I'm not saying that I like it, but I plan to honor your wishes."

"Actually, I've been considering something, too."

That it would be a cold day in hell before she got in his bed, he decided. "What?"

"I'm beginning to feel closer to you, too. So maybe we'll be ready sooner than we think."

At the moment, Drew was more than ready. He closed his eyes and saw only her, imagined her beside him. Beneath him. "I wish you were here now," he said.

"That would be nice."

His ensuing laugh held no humor. "What I'm thinking isn't nice at all."

"Just what are you thinking, Drew Connelly?" Her voice was a mix of amusement and challenge.

"I'm thinking that if you were here, I'd have you in this bed with me so we could go camping."

"Would you care to explain that?"

"There's a pup tent under the sheets."

She released a soft laugh. "Oh, so that's my fault, is it?"

"You've got that right. Just listening to your voice makes me hard as a boulder." He'd probably gone too far with that revelation, but surprisingly, she laughed again.

"I'm so sorry you're in such a predicament, Mr. Connelly. I'm also sorry I can't help you out with that."

So was he, aching with remorse. "You *could* help me out."

"Drew, you're not proposing phone sex, are you?"

"Computer sex? I have my laptop."

"I'm afraid I'm a little too inhibited for that."

"I'm kidding, Kristina. When this happens between us, I want you with me. I want to be able to see you when I touch you. I want to see you the moment you go over the edge, and babe, I plan to take you there."

"Wow."

Wow was right, and a definite understatement. If Drew didn't stop now, he was in danger of disregarding his business and hopping the next plane to take care of other more pressing business.

"Until that time," he said, "I'll just have to live with my fantasies." And the tent.

"That goes both ways," she said followed by a long sigh.

"Sweet dreams, Kristina. I'll see you tomorrow night."

"I'll be here."

With that she hung up, leaving Drew alone with his desire along with a heady excitement brought about by the fact she would be waiting for him when he returned home.

It also brought on some heavy apprehension, fear of the feelings for Kristina that had begun to creep to the surface, up past the emotional armor. Fear that he might not be able to live up to her expectations.

But for the first time in five sorry years, he felt truly alive, thanks to Kristina Simmons.

It suddenly occurred to him that his mind had somehow started to change, along with his plans. Maybe he should give the relationship his best shot. Maybe he could open himself up to all the possibilities, try to work through the many mistakes he'd made with Talia and not repeat them with Kristina. What did he have to lose?

He knew the answer to that. Once Kristina learned the truth about how the engagement came to be, he could very well lose her.

Eventually he would have to tell her the honest-to-God truth, after he had proved to her, and to himself, that he could perhaps be the man she needed.

"He's here, Kristina!" Mandy hurried away from the window and joined Kristina on the piano bench.

Kristina couldn't halt the thrill over knowing Drew was about to walk through the door after four days. He'd called a half hour ago to tell them he'd be stopping by to pick up his own car and to say hello before heading to the office. He wouldn't be home for very long, but the prospect of spending ten minutes in his presence had Kristina reeling from anticipation.

Their conversation the night before, when Drew had promised pleasure, made Kristina suddenly impatient to be alone with him again. Yet with Mandy in the house, she doubted that would happen any time soon.

It might, this weekend, in the woods. Heavens, she was definitely becoming a naughty girl, thanks to Mr. Connelly.

But right now she had to concentrate on Mandy and her surprise. "Are you ready, honey?"

Amanda gave a definite nod of her head and placed her tiny fingers on the keys. "I'm ready, Freddy."

"Okay. I think I just heard the door open."

"I'm home, you two," Drew called out, his deep voice echoing in the foyer beyond the room.

"We're in the piano room, Daddy!" Mandy called back.

The sound of approaching footsteps caused Mandy to start squirming. Kristina couldn't blame her. She wanted to squirm, too. Instead, she counted in eight-time, signaling Mandy to begin playing the moment Drew walked in.

Maybe it wasn't the greatest rendition of "Mary Had a Little Lamb," but you couldn't tell that from the look of pride on Drew's face. Yet the pride was soon replaced by a hint of sorrow, brought on by memories of his wife, Kristina assumed.

That in itself could keep Drew from making a real commitment to her. Perhaps he only wanted her for the sex, something she would have to think about later, after he left once again. She couldn't think at all with him standing there, looking so darned handsome she considered throwing herself into his arms.

When Mandy stopped playing, Drew approached and braced one hip against the piano. "That was awesome, Mandy."

Amanda beamed like the crystal chandelier hanging above them. "You liked it, Daddy?"

He walked behind Mandy and pulled her off the bench, then up into his arms. "I loved it."

When Mandy wrapped her arms around Drew's neck, he looked at Kristina over Mandy's head. "Thanks. This was a great surprise."

After he settled Mandy back on her feet, she stared up at him, grinning ear to ear. "What did you get me, Daddy?"

"It's in the hall. Blue sack."

Mandy sprinted out of the room as fast as her little feet would allow her.

An awkward silence hung over the room while Kristina

waited for Drew to do something, say something. Finally he held out his hand for her to take. She rose and walked easily into his arms despite her earlier concerns. He hugged her tightly, unearthing more hope from deep within her. Maybe he had missed her as much as she'd missed him.

Pulling back, he settled his gaze on her eyes. "You think you could manage a welcome-home kiss for this weary traveler?"

"I guess I could." She pointed to her cheek. "Right here, Big Daddy," she said, parroting Mandy.

He gave her a mock scowl that quickly turned into a deadly grin. "Not at all what I had in mind." Not Kristina either, but she knew Mandy would be back soon.

As if Drew realized that as well, he kissed her softly, no more than a light touch of their lips, but warmth flowed through Kristina in response to the tender gesture.

"It's so beautiful, Daddy!"

Kristina stepped away from Drew and turned her attention to Mandy who stood holding a package in one hand and a miniature music-box piano in the other.

"That is beautiful, Drew," Kristina said.

"You did good, Daddy-O." Mandy held up the other box. "Is this for me?"

Drew snatched it from her hand. "It's for Kristina. She can open it later."

Mandy screwed up her face into a frown. "I want to see her open it."

"Not now, Mandy." He leveled his gaze on Kristina. "I want her to open it later, when I come back home."

First the gentle kiss, now the surprise gift. Kristina's worries drifted away like the dust specks floating on the stream of light that spilled across Drew's broad shoulders. He looked so gorgeous, backlit by the setting sun.

He would probably look beautiful cloaked in darkness. One night she might find out.

Discarding that thought, Kristina walked to Mandy and took the music box, giving herself someplace to look so she wouldn't stare at Drew. "Why don't you put this on your shelf, then finish that picture you colored for Daddy?"

"Okay." Mandy started away again but reconsidered. "Don't go until I bring you the picture, Daddy."

Drew glanced at his watch. "You can give it to me later. Right now I have to meet your grandfather at the office and give my report."

"Daaaaddy," Mandy whined. "You're always gone."

"I know, sweetheart, but I'll be back. Now go on up to your room and I'll see you later."

"I'm always going to my room," Mandy murmured on her way out.

Drew handed the box to Kristina. "Here. Open it now before she shows up again."

Kristina stared at the red paisley package. "I'm almost afraid to open it."

Drew grinned. "I promise it won't bite. Though I might if you wear it."

She had no doubt what was in the box, but she did have doubts over whether she'd like it. Her doubts increased tenfold when she placed the box on the piano bench and opened it to find a black lace nightgown, if one could call it that. It was more like a short strip of sheerness with straps.

Holding it up to the window, Kristina gasped. It looked even skimpier in the light. "Drew, I'm not sure I can wear this."

He came up behind her and circled his arms around her waist. "Oh, I think you can, and quite well. It's an original, created from some of our very own lace."

And probably very expensive, Kristina decided. "I'll think about it."

He pushed her hair aside and brought his lips to her ear, his warm breath playing over her neck, playing havoc on her body. "Don't think about it. Just do it."

She leaned back against his solid chest, lost in the feel of him against her, and she could feel everything. *Everything.*

He was aroused, but then so was she. Very aroused. So much so that she turned into his arms and kissed him the way she'd wanted to when he'd entered the room. The way she'd wanted to every hour of every day since he'd been gone.

The gown dropped to the floor and Drew's hands dropped to her hips. He pulled her forward and his erection nudged her belly, caused her breath to disappear, along with any and every reservation about making love with him.

He moved back a step, taking her with him, but she wasn't sure where they were heading. At the moment she didn't care.

The tinkling sound of piano keys rang out in the empty room as Drew's behind backed up into the instrument. Drew broke the kiss and his gaze cut to the piano.

The pain on his face sliced through the fog of desire that had clouded Kristina's judgment. He might as well have dunked her in a trough of ice water. On the other hand, Drew looked as if he'd been burned. As far as Kristina was concerned, he had been burned. By his memories.

The stifling silence continued for a long moment until he finally said, "We can't do this here."

Kristina took a much-needed step back. "I understand."

His blue eyes were full of despair that he tried to cloak

with a smile. "I mean, we shouldn't do this now. Amanda's upstairs and she might be coming down soon. I've got to go."

"You're right. Otherwise you might miss dinner."

"I won't be here for dinner."

"Really? Where will you be?" She sounded ridiculously jealous, as if he might find another woman to take care of his needs, when in fact she was competing with a ghost.

"I'll be at work," he said, his tone frustrated. "Where else would I be?"

"Of course you'll be at work." She lowered her eyes. "I'll see you when you get home."

Without a word, he left her alone once again. Left her with the worry that she might never be more than a means to an end, sex for the sake of gratification. A way for him to forget the woman he'd loved—probably still loved—at least until the memories came back to him as they had a few moments before.

She wanted to be more to him than a diversion. She wanted to be everything. She wouldn't settle for anything less.

Drew closed the front door quietly behind him, hoping not to alert anyone that he was home. He headed upstairs to covertly check on his daughter, then he planned to have a good long talk with Kristina.

His plan went awry when he didn't find Mandy in her bed. Heading back down the stairs, he made his way to Kristina's room and slowly opened the door.

What he saw clamped his heart in an imaginary vise.

The bedside lamp was still on, casting Kristina's beautiful face in shadows. Mandy was curled up beside her, fast asleep, looking peaceful, content, totally happy.

Drew struggled with the need to wake Kristina. He

wanted to apologize to her for the way he'd acted in the music room. It wasn't as if he'd considered himself cheating on Talia with Kristina. He was simply reminded that he had cheated Talia of so many things, and he didn't want to rob Kristina of a chance to be happy. He couldn't make her happy unless he knew for certain that he was ready to commit.

Maybe this weekend he'd have the opportunity to really talk to her. Then again, with his family around, he might not have a moment alone with her at all.

He'd have to try and get Kristina alone. Then somehow, someway, he had to convince her that this was more than sex brewing between them. He cared for her more than he'd ever thought possible. Maybe even more than he could handle.

He leaned down and kissed his daughter's cheek, then took a chance and kissed Kristina, too.

Neither of them stirred, allowing him to watch them a little longer. Seeing Kristina cuddled up with his daughter, looking like a mother, brought about more concerns over her burgeoning relationship with Mandy. A great thing under normal circumstances, but these circumstances were anything but normal.

This relationship with Kristina had begun as a scheme he'd had no part in, yet Drew suddenly realized it was beginning to develop into much, much more. He could talk business with the best, work a deal on a moment's notice, but he had little knowledge on how to negotiate matters of the heart.

He had a lot to contend with, and far too little time.

Six

If this was Drew Connelly's idea of a cabin, then Kristina could be a supermodel.

The rear of the majestic log home spanned the length of a wooded area beyond the tree-lined driveway. Varying pitches to the slate-colored roof, twin chimneys on opposite ends, a large deck and several balconies set it apart from any *cabin* Kristina had ever seen before. The lake gleamed in the Wisconsin summer sun hovering over the west horizon, as blue as Drew's eyes that now studied her while he remained behind the wheel. He looked pleased and proud, and Kristina couldn't fault him for that.

"Drew, this is beautiful," she said, staring at the home in disbelief. "You and Brett really built this?"

"We did most of it, but we did have some help."

"I'm impressed."

"So am I."

She brought her gaze from the house back to Drew and found him staring at her, his expression suddenly serious, his eyes now centered on her mouth as if he might actually kiss her.

"Are we there yet, Daddy?"

Mandy's sleepy voice pulled Drew's attention to the back seat. "Yeah, we're there, sweetheart."

Kristina looked back to find Mandy fumbling for the seat belt then watched as she tore out of the SUV like a tiny tempest. Kristina visually followed her progress and suddenly noted two people standing on the back porch, looking expectant.

Drew sighed. "The welcoming committee has arrived."

"Then I guess we'd better get out now." The disappointment in her voice surprised Kristina. She looked forward to meeting Drew's family, but she wasn't looking forward to having so little time alone with Drew. She had many things she wanted to discuss with him, but because of his late arrival home the night before, the preparations that morning for the trip, and with Amanda awake most of the drive, the opportunity hadn't presented itself.

Drew seemed in no hurry to exit as he draped his arm around her shoulder and pulled her closer. "Guess it's time to face the jury."

Kristina frowned. "Now, that encourages me to get out."

"Don't worry. They're not that bad." He ran a fingertip along her jaw. "Maybe we should sneak a little kiss. That ought to convince them."

"Convince them of what?"

Drew's gaze slid away. "Convince them to leave early so we can be alone."

Drew hadn't sounded all that believable to Kristina.

Perhaps he thought that after his family saw her, he would have to work extra hard to persuade them that he was interested in a plain country schoolteacher from Wisconsin with roots firmly embedded in a farming heritage.

He smiled, lessening some of her apprehension. "Are you ready?"

"Okay. I'm sure they're probably wondering where we are."

"That's not what I meant." His voice had a grainy quality about it, rough yet seductive.

"Then what did you mean?"

"I meant, are you ready for this?" He took her right arm and draped it over his shoulder then gave her a kiss that could fell the nearby trees. Kristina was definitely falling fast with each foray of his gentle tongue into her eager mouth, the pulse of desire spreading throughout her entire being. Sliding his hand up from her waist, he ran his thumb back and forth along the side of her breast. The strong afternoon sun filtering through the windshield was nothing compared to the fire building within her from his kiss, his touch.

The kiss grew deeper, his fingertips moving closer to dangerous ground, and the moan that rose up in Kristina's throat took her totally by surprise.

Mortified, Kristina pulled away and leaned back against the seat, her breath coming out in labored puffs. "I don't think that qualifies as a 'little' kiss, Mr. Connelly. I have a reputation to uphold with your family, and I doubt making out with you in an SUV will aid me in that cause."

Drew leaned his head back against the seat and expelled a ragged breath. "Yeah, guess you're right."

She opened the door and slid out of the truck but when she leaned back inside to retrieve her purse, she noticed that Drew had yet to move. "Are you going to make me go by myself?"

He turned his face toward her and shifted in his seat. "Give me just a minute, okay?"

"Are you that worried about what your parents are going to think of me?"

A chuckle erupted from low in his chest. "I'm worried about what they're going to think of me. If I don't pull myself together, I'm going to embarrass us both."

Kristina's gaze dropped to his lap where she immediately viewed the extent of his problem beneath his khaki shorts. "Oh. I see."

"Yeah, and so will my mother. Not a good idea."

Her knees suddenly felt feeble, so she grabbed the open door for support. "Should I go ahead and make up some kind of excuse for your delay?"

His grin came halfway, looked cynical. "What would that be? Drew's in the truck and any minute now you'll hear him honk the horn without his hands?"

Kristina laughed then. She couldn't stop it. She also couldn't stop the exhilaration over knowing she had been responsible for his predicament. "I'll wait for you."

"Might be a while, unless we take out all the luggage and climb in back to take care of my little problem."

Drew obviously had a skewed view of proportions. His current problem didn't look "little" by any means, not that Kristina had anything to compare it to.

Feeling just a bit too wicked, a bit too willing to prolong the tension, Kristina leaned forward and braced her palms on the seat. "A tailgate party might be fun."

Drew's gaze came to rest on the cleavage revealed by the scoop neck of her sundress. "I wish you had worn something less distracting, like maybe a turtleneck."

"It's a little warm for that, don't you think?"

His gaze continued to linger on her breasts. "Actually, it's way too hot at the moment because of that dress. Now I might never be able to get out."

"Oh, but dresses make quickies so much more convenient."

He groaned. "You're not helping me, Kristina."

She straightened and smiled. "Maybe I can 'help you' a little later."

With that, she headed to the back of the SUV and raised the tailgate, thinking that her inhibitions had not come on this vacation with her, thanks to Drew. She needed to take a step back, remember that before she decided to execute that all-important leap of faith, she had to be sure that something other than chemistry existed between them. Something deeper, an emotional connection they could build on. She had to know for a fact that he was ready to put the past behind him and start anew—with her.

She hadn't forgotten his demands, either, although she suspected he'd been teasing her since he hadn't brought them up again. In fact, he'd even helped her with the dishes the other night without her asking. She supposed that if he made her haul the luggage by herself, then that would prove he'd added pack mule to his list.

By the time Kristina had grabbed two of the bags from the back of the truck, Drew joined her. She couldn't stop her gaze from traveling downward to see if his problem had disappeared. It hadn't, not completely. She shoved her tote with the shoulder strap at him, coming dangerously close to the affected area of his body. "Here. Hang this around your neck."

"Don't start, Kristina," he said with a mock warning tone.

She laid a hand on her chest. "I have no idea what you're talking about."

His gaze shot to her hand resting on her breast and he quickly looked away. "You know exactly what you're doing, Ms. Simmons."

At times she wondered if she really did. Drew Connelly had a knack for making her disregard good judgment. But he was so cute in his beige shirt and those great shorts that revealed his toned, tanned legs. And what a remarkable butt, she thought as he leaned over and took out Amanda's suitcase. At least it appeared she wouldn't have to carry everything. It also appeared that she would have to work extra hard to keep her eyes to herself this weekend, lest she get caught looking at private places she had no business looking at in public.

Drew slipped the tote's strap over one shoulder and clutched Amanda's suitcase in one hand. "Let's go."

"I'm with you." And she longed to be with him in every way, despite her need to be cautious. Her need for Drew was beginning to outweigh everything, a very scary concept.

"They don't know about the e-mail thing," he murmured as they started up the walkway to the porch, now hand in hand. "They think we met at a singles' bar."

"Oh, great," Kristina said quietly. One huge strike against her.

Once they reached the porch, Amanda rushed over and pulled Kristina's hand from Drew's. "Isn't she pretty, Grandmother?"

"Very pretty indeed," the elegant woman said, her hand outstretched for Kristina to take. "I'm Emma, Drew's mother. We're so pleased to meet you, Kristina." After Kristina shook her hand, Emma gestured toward the debonair man standing beside her. "Drew's father, Grant."

"Likewise," Grant said, favoring her with another handshake and a smile much like Drew's.

"It's so nice to meet you both," Kristina said, feeling relieved enough to smile since they sounded sincere.

"Don't just stand there. Get over here and give me a proper welcome, Amanda Elizabeth."

Kristina looked beyond Drew's parents to see a petite and somewhat frail woman with cotton-colored hair standing near the door, one hand braced on a cane. Amanda rushed over and gave her a gentle hug. "Nana Lilly! I brought Kristina."

Lilly shuffled her way over to Kristina and looked her up and down. "My, my. You are a lovely little thing."

Little thing? Obviously the whole family was size-challenged. "Thank you, Lilly. It's good to meet you, too."

Lilly poked her cane at Drew. "You've done very well, Grandson."

Looking self-conscious, Drew slipped his hands into the pockets of his shorts. "Thanks, Grandmother."

Amanda tugged on her father's arm, gaining his attention. "I saw you and Kristina kissing in the car." She sounded as though she'd just discovered buried treasure.

Emma's lips curled into a smile and Grant studied his shoe.

Drew tried to appear nonchalant, but the uneasiness in his eyes was all too obvious. "We were talking, Mandy."

"Speaking in tongues, no doubt," Lilly said with a wicked smile.

"Behave yourself, Mother," Grant cautioned.

"Oh, posh. There's no fun in that, right, Drew?" Without awaiting a response, Lilly turned to the door. "Come inside, everyone. Dinner is served. Rosie has truly out-done herself this time.''

Lilly held open the door, allowing everyone to pass through except Kristina and Drew. When Kristina tried to enter, Lilly stopped her by laying a hand on her arm. "Wait a moment, young lady. I'd like to have a word with you."

Drew came up from behind Kristina and gave Lilly a warning look. "Grandmother, Kristina's tired from the drive. Can't this wait?"

Lilly's eyes softened with understanding. "Of course it can wait. Until after we eat. Then we'll have a nice talk."

Kristina had no idea what that might entail, but she decided to prepare for anything.

Drew was surrounded by his close-knit family, but he could only concentrate on one member of the dinner party—Kristina.

He'd never before been so intrigued by watching someone eat. Talk. Laugh.

Kristina had done all of that, and by the attentive looks on his family's faces, they were totally taken with her, just as he'd suspected. He could definitely relate.

"I'm afraid most of the children won't be here to-morrow, Kristina," Emma said with a delicate dab of her napkin on her chin. "Maura and Doug will be for certain, but everyone else seems to be busy. Tara won't be com-ing. Little Brandon's under the weather with a summer cold, so she decided to keep him in the city." She di-rected her smile at Kristina. "Tara and her son live with us in town."

"How wonderful for you," Kristina said enthusiasti-cally.

"It's fine if they can't come, Mother," Drew replied. "Kristina will eventually meet them all." And as far as Drew was concerned, the lack of relatives made for better odds of getting Kristina alone.

He did question whether Tara's decision to stay in town had to do with someone following her, or if she simply didn't want to be around the family. Since the death of her husband, she'd changed, very unlike the girl he'd grown up with, appropriately labeled Tara the Terrible. She'd been fun-loving and gregarious. Now, for the most part, she was moody and withdrawn.

He hadn't had a chance to speak with Tara yet, and he assumed she hadn't told the family about her concerns since neither Grant nor Emma seemed worried. At least Tara would be safe at the manor on Lake Shore. Fort Knox couldn't hold up in comparison.

"Tobias will be joining us tomorrow," Lilly added. "He was playing in a seniors golf tournament today. Of course, he'll be worn to a frazzle with a sunburned head."

"I look forward to seeing him again," Kristina said.

Emma sat forward. "Again?"

"Yes, we met at Drew's the first day I—" Color rose high in Kristina's cheek, and Drew held his breath. "The day I moved my things into the house."

"The day she came to be my mommy," Mandy announced.

Drew was really beginning to sweat now. One slip from Mandy and the whole charade would be blown wide open. He didn't want Kristina to learn everything in front of his family, nor did he want his family to know about the true circumstances behind how they met.

Lilly pushed back her chair and stood. "Come along, Amanda dear. I'll help you get ready for your bath."

Obviously Lilly was trying to cover her own role in the farce, Drew thought.

"Let me do it, Lilly," Emma said, rising like an elegant mist from her chair. "I spend far too little time with Amanda these days."

"Can't Kristina come, too?" Mandy asked.

"I need to talk with Kristina, dear heart," Lilly said. "You run along with your grandmother and get ready for bed."

Great. That was all Drew needed, his grandmother revealing God only knew what to Kristina. But he knew better than to cross Lilly Connelly. He could only hope that she was judicious in what she said to Kristina, especially when it came to personal details about Drew's history. Some things were best left buried in the past.

Grant sat forward and pushed back his plate. "If you're finished now, son, why don't you join me in the study for a moment?"

"You promised you wouldn't talk business," Emma scolded as she headed away with Amanda.

"It's not exactly business," Grant called after her then turned his attention to Drew. "But it is important."

"Sure, Dad. If it's important." Drew doubted he could focus on much of anything, important or not, knowing that Lilly had already piloted Kristina away for "the talk."

Drew reluctantly followed his dad out of the dining room, past the great room and into the first-floor study that held two desks, one for Drew and one for Brett. Just when they'd each settled on one of the leather sofas in the corner, the front doorbell rang.

"That must be them," Grant said, heading for the door.

Drew stood and said, "Who?" but his father ignored the query. Drew hoped it wasn't some associate, or some friend's kid seeking employment at Connelly Corporation. He didn't have the energy to deal with that at present. The only thing he wanted to deal with was Kristina, and in a manner that would be considered totally inappropriate by his family.

A few moments later, Grant reentered the room with Tom Reynolds and Lucas Starwind, the detectives looking into the attempt on Daniel's life. Must be serious business, Drew thought. He hoped his brother hadn't suffered through another threat. But he suspected it was very serious, otherwise they wouldn't have come all the way to the lake at this time of night.

"Have a seat," Grant said as he made his way to the wet bar in the corner. "Scotch anyone?"

Drew was tempted to accept but decided against it. Liquor would probably go straight to his head, and Kristina was already doing a good job at keeping him drunk with anticipation. "No, thanks, Dad," he said as he settled back onto the sofa.

Reynolds hitched up his pants over the slight paunch of his belly then sank into the sofa opposite Drew. "None for me, but thanks."

"None for me, either," Starwind said, seating himself on the edge of a lounger chair near the fireplace, sporting his usual all-business expression.

Grant rejoined them holding a half-full glass of Scotch, straight up. He took a long drink then said, "Well?"

"We've got some news," Reynolds began. "Seems Angie Donahue has ties to Jimmy Kelly. He's her uncle."

Drew winced over hearing both names. Angie Donahue was a subject no one brought up often in the family. Grant had been involved with Angie when he and Emma were having marital problems a number of years ago, a detail Drew hadn't known until adulthood.

From that brief affair, Drew's half brother Seth was born. Angie hadn't been a good mother and had turned Seth over to Grant to raise when the boy was twelve years old. And now Angie was haunting them again, and on top of that, tied to an infamous crime family.

How was that going to affect Seth once he learned the truth? And how was Emma going to take the news?

Drew had always admired his mother for accepting a child that wasn't hers, a product of her husband's extra-marital affair. Admired her forgiveness of his father's indiscretion. Some might think her a fool, but Drew only had to view the glances between his mother and father to realize that unconditional love bound them together, despite the hardships.

He wondered if Kristina would be that forgiving once she learned about his grandmother's scheming, and his own withholding of the truth. Could he ever hope to have the kind of love that existed between his parents?

"...this is a solid lead?"

Drew snapped back into reality when he realized his father was speaking. He'd probably missed damned near most of the conversation.

"We won't know until we investigate further," Luke offered.

"Anything else on Charlotte?" Grant asked.

"Nothing more than what we told you earlier," Reynolds said. "But we're still keeping an eye on her. We'll let you know if anything else comes up."

This was much too bizarre for Drew's liking, and made him that much more determined to keep Mandy and Kristina safe. He didn't exactly believe they were in danger, but he wasn't going to take that risk. Until this whole thing was resolved, he'd make sure that he maintained tight security at the house.

Grant rose, signaling the meeting was now over. The

other men took his cue and stood. Thankful for that, Drew followed all three to the front door.

Reynolds walked out into the night but Starwind hung back. He handed Grant a piece of paper. "Just thought I'd let you know that I'm going to be leaving town on a personal emergency. That's the number where you can reach me."

"Reynolds will be around, right?" Grant asked.

Starwind streaked a hand over his jaw. "Yeah, but he has a tendency to go off on his own to chase down leads that might be potentially dangerous. If he tells you anything, call me because I know he won't."

As Starwind headed down the front steps, Grant said, "Consider it done," then closed the door.

Grant turned and patted Drew on the back. "Come have a drink with me, son, and I'll fill you in on all the investigation details since you seemed to be a bit distracted. And we could talk a little business, as long as your mother is occupied with Amanda."

Drew didn't want to talk business. He wanted to know what Kristina was doing now. More accurately, what Lilly was saying to Kristina.

"I really should help clean up," Kristina said, feeling like a slug sitting in the small garden room situated at the rear of the house, sipping a glass of sherry when she should be doing her part.

"That's what Rosie's for," Lilly said. "She's the caretaker's wife. She looks after both Drew's lake house and the Connelly lake cottage. A nice lady. Almost part of the family."

Kristina had begun to feel a part of the family, although that might not be wise considering her relationship with Drew was still very tenuous.

Lilly leaned forward in the club chair, both hands

braced on the cane. "My grandson can be a tough character," she began. "He's been through quite a bit."

Kristina welcomed the chance to learn more about Drew. "I'm sure losing his wife was quite a blow. I assume she was very young."

"He hasn't spoken to you about Talia?"

Kristina shrugged. "Only a little. I know that she died when Amanda was a baby."

"Then you don't know why she died?"

"I don't even know *how* she died."

Lilly settled back in the chair. "Very tragic, really. A prescription-drug overdose."

Kristina stifled a gasp. "Was it a—I mean, did she—"

"Take her own life? In a manner of speaking, but no one believes it was intentional, only an unfortunate lack of judgment on Talia's part. However, she was depressed after Amanda was born and quite frankly, she was always very frail. Add that to the loss of her career, it's understandable she would be overwhelmed."

"What career?"

Lilly sighed. "Talia was a gifted pianist, studied at Juilliard. When she became pregnant, Drew married her and that was the end of that."

Everything was beginning to become very clear to Kristina. No wonder Drew had reacted so strongly when he'd found her playing his wife's piano. "He still misses her very much."

"He's eaten up by guilt," Lilly said. "They were both too young. Drew still blames himself for saddling her with a baby when neither of them was ready. He won't say as much, but grandmothers know these things."

"He certainly seems to love Amanda."

Lilly sent her a fond smile. "Oh, heavens, yes. He thinks the sun rises and sets in that child. She's his touchstone, I tell you. But she's also been his excuse not to open himself up to finding real love with a woman. He thinks that loving Amanda is enough for him. Or he did until you came along.''

Kristina suddenly felt like a fraud. If only Lilly knew how this whole engagement came about. Drew might want her, but Kristina feared it had nothing to do with love. She had no choice but to be forthcoming with the truth, even knowing Drew probably wouldn't approve. But after Lilly had been so open with her, she deserved the whole story.

Kristina inhaled a deep breath. ''To be perfectly honest, Drew and I met over the Internet, through e-mails.''

''E-mails?'' Lilly's smile deepened, catching Kristina off guard. ''I suppose that's something along the lines of being a mail-order bride, and in my day, that was a common occurrence. It was also common that a deep abiding love came from that circumstance. Communication is certainly the key to a solid relationship.''

If only Kristina could convince Drew to communicate with her. She was only beginning to understand the scope of his pain. She wanted to know more, perhaps even help him to heal. ''Well, this engagement is a trial run, so to speak. I hope that love comes out of it.''

''It already has,'' Lilly said, her keen blue eyes leveled on Kristina. ''You are in love with him, aren't you?''

That realization settled on Kristina's heart like a leaden weight. ''I suppose I could be.'' More than likely she was.

''And he's in love with you, too,'' Lilly stated. ''He just doesn't know it yet. But he will, in time.''

Kristina sighed. ''Oh, Lilly, I wish I could believe that, but he's still hurting over his wife's death. I don't know how to reach him.''

Lilly rested a careworn hand on Kristina's arm. ''I'll tell you exactly how to do it. Men are different creatures.

In order to have the love, they have to have affection first, if you know what I mean.''

Kristina knew exactly what she meant, or at least she thought she did. ''Are you referring to sex?''

''Of course. Shocking, I suppose, but true. Women want the emotions in order to have sex. Men can't have the emotions until they can get their minds off their Johnsons.''

Kristina worried her bottom lip. ''Then you're saying that I should—''

''Explore the possibility, and enjoy the journey. That's exactly how I caught my Tobias.''

A chuckle bubbled up in Kristina's throat then came out in a full-fledged laugh.

''What's so funny, you two?''

Kristina's laughter halted at the sound of Drew's voice coming from behind her. She turned to see him propped against the door frame, questions and concerns reflecting in his eyes.

Lilly stood gingerly. ''Nothing you should worry about, beloved.''

Without a word, Drew pushed off the frame. ''Do you want me to round everyone up so you can head back to the cottage, Grandmother?''

Lilly rested one hand on her cane. ''Did Grant not tell you?''

Drew frowned. ''Tell me what?''

''We're staying here tonight. Emma had the master bedroom repainted at the cottage, and she said the fumes give her a headache. Of course, I told her a few fumes didn't hurt anyone. But she's determined to wait until tomorrow to return, so I'm afraid we're your guests for the night.''

Kristina immediately noticed the displeasure in Drew's expression. ''I can sleep on the sofa,'' she offered.

"Nonsense," Lilly said. "There are four bedrooms. Grant and Emma can take Brett's room, you can take Drew's. Amanda has her own room and that leaves the daybed in the guest room for me."

"And where am I supposed to sleep?" Drew asked.

Lilly's smile appeared slowly. "I suppose you'll have to figure that out." She turned to Kristina. "Give me a hug, my dear. I'm taking this old tired body to bed."

Kristina rose from her chair and accepted the embrace. Before she let Lilly go, she whispered, "Thank you."

Lilly drew back and said, "No. Thank you. You have a good soul, Kristina Simmons, and a kind heart." She gave Drew a meaningful look. "A perfect match for my grandson, I do believe."

She headed away and without turning around said, "Pleasant dreams, you two, or whatever you might find pleasant tonight."

A slow heat started at Kristina's throat then traveled all the way to her hairline. As tempting as the thought might be, she couldn't sleep with Drew in the house with his family on the premises. "Really, Drew, I don't mind sleeping on the couch." She snapped her fingers. "Or I could sleep with Mandy."

"The bed's a twin," Drew said. "Besides, I just went to check on her. She's already out." He sighed. "I should've suspected this when everyone suddenly disappeared. Would've been nice if someone had told me."

Kristina was feeling a bit disappointed that Drew hadn't even suggested they sleep together. He could have at least offered. "If you're sure, I guess I'll head to bed. You'll have to show me the way."

Drew's slow-burn smile suddenly appeared. "I'd like nothing better than to show you the way."

She backed up when he stalked toward her. "Hold it right there, buster. You have to be good."

He caught up to her and wrapped his arms around her waist, then pulled her to him. "I plan to be good."

"I mean it, Drew." She didn't sound at all like she meant it, especially since Drew now had his face buried in her neck.

He gave her a brushstroke kiss on her lips. "While you're all cozy in my king-size bed, just remember me while I'm laid out on the sofa with a king-size h—"

She slapped a palm over his mouth. "Do you want someone to hear you?"

He tugged her hand away then slid the tip of his tongue across her palm. "I was going to say headache. King-size headache."

Kristina couldn't keep from smiling. "Oh, I'm so sure."

Taking her by the shoulders, he turned her around and patted her bottom. "Up the stairs, to the right, at the end of the hall. It has an adjoining bathroom with a whirlpool. Have fun."

Kristina headed toward the staircase thinking she wouldn't have any fun without Drew.

When he called her name, she looked back over her shoulder. "Yes?"

He gave her a full-throttle grin. "You look as good in back as you do in front."

"Go to bed, Drew."

"I will. But you can bet I'll probably be camping."

Seven

As Drew predicted, he couldn't sleep to save his life. The couch was too small, and his need for Kristina too great. He couldn't even toss and turn without toppling over the edge.

This wasn't going to work, he thought as he sat up and braced both hands on his neck already stiff from the position he'd maintained for over two hours. That wasn't the only thing.

Kristina kept playing through his mind like a favorite song. He couldn't seem to stop thinking about her, thinking about what he'd like to do with her.

Maybe he should go to her. After all, his bed was more than adequate for both of them. Besides, they didn't have to do anything other than hold each other.

Might work at that. He had nothing to lose by trying, except maybe control. Nope, he'd just have to be strong, keep his hands to himself. He didn't even have to wake her. He could just crawl in and be content knowing she was nearby, knowing he couldn't touch her the way he really wanted to, at least not tonight. Then he could sneak back to the couch before dawn.

Slipping on his shorts and shirt, he took the stairs two at a time as quietly as he could. Once he arrived at his room, he pushed open the door that creaked too loudly. He waited for a moment to see if he'd alerted Kristina to his presence. The last thing he needed was to scare her to death.

He couldn't make out much in the limited light other than Kristina's form beneath the covers. She hadn't seemed to move. So far, so good. He immediately knocked his toe on the edge of the lounger near the door. Stifling a string of curses, he managed to arrive at the bed without ramming any more obstacles.

Quietly he undressed down to his briefs and braced his knee on the mattress that groaned beneath his weight.

The mound of covers moved and Drew hated that he'd wakened her. "It's me, Kristina."

"Guess again."

"What the—?" Drew bolted from the bed, grabbed for his shorts and tugged them back on with fumbling fingers. "Grandmother?"

"An astute observation, dear Drew."

He choked down a foul curse. "What are you doing here?"

The bedside lamp flipped on, revealing Lilly's rheumy eyes trying to focus, a sour look on her face. "For your information, your fiancée is in the guest room. She insisted I take your bed so I'd be more comfortable."

Drew was anything but comfortable at the moment having been caught by his grandmother with his pants down, literally. He pulled on his shirt and said, "Actually, I…'' What excuse could he possibly give Lilly that sounded remotely believable?

Lilly sat up on the edge of the bed and yawned. "I know what you're up to, Grandson."

"I just wanted to tell her good-night."

"Without your clothes?" Lilly glanced at the bedside clock. "And it's a little late for conversation." She let go a grating chuckle.

"I couldn't sleep," he said. "I thought she might want to talk."

"You thought no such thing." Lilly settled herself back into bed and flipped a hand toward the door. "Go find her. Your secret's safe with me."

So much for his plan to crawl in the sack with Kristina. The daybed in the guest room wouldn't allow enough space for both of them, at least not side by side. On the other hand…

That was the last thing he needed to imagine at the moment with Lilly staring at him expectantly. "Good night, Grandmother. Sorry I woke you." He pivoted toward the door.

"One more thing, Drew."

So much for a quick escape. "What?" he asked, not bothering to turn around.

"Kristina is a fine young woman, and she deserves your respect. If you don't have any intention of seeing this through beyond a quick tumble between the sheets, then you'd best think twice."

Finally he faced her. "I understand what you're saying, Grandmother. But I have to admit, I do like her. A lot." Drew was surprised at how easily the confession rolled off his tongue.

Lilly smiled with satisfaction. "Of course you like her. Grandmother always knows best. You may thank me later.'' With that, she snapped off the light and Drew walked out the door, her words echoing in his mind.

He did like Kristina, more than he ever thought he would. And he certainly didn't want to hurt her. He wanted to be with her, talk to her, hold her, and no doubt about it, make love to her. Maybe even tell her things he'd never told any woman, told anyone for that matter. He hoped he would have that opportunity soon, if not tonight.

Halfway down the stairs on his return to the dreaded sofa, Drew reconsidered and paused at the window on the landing. A half-moon cut a swath of light across the glass-still lake, bringing with it a great idea.

The cove. Kristina. A place to be alone.

He ran the risk that Kristina might not agree to come with him, but he could tell her that he wanted to go for a midnight stroll, away from his family's prying eyes, especially Lilly's. To allow them the chance to talk, relax, and whatever else might transpire in the dark of night.

All he could do was ask, and hope that he didn't find someone other than Kristina in the guest-room bed.

"Kristina.''

The sultry voice pulled Kristina from her momentary dozing. For hours she'd been awake, thinking about Drew, and now, as if she'd conjured him up, he was stroking her hair and speaking to her in soft whispers.

She rolled to face him, her heart filled with joy over his sudden presence. "Can't sleep?'' she asked.

"Not a bit. How about you?''

"Not much.''

"Care to go exploring?''

She pushed herself up to a sitting position. "Drew, your parents are right next door."

"Not here."

"Then where?"

He stood and held out his hand. "Outside. I have a place I want to show you."

Kristina wondered what else he wanted to show her once they arrived at the place. That consideration brought about an overwhelming excitement. She draped her legs over the edge of the bed and sat up. "I need to change."

"No, you don't. Just put on some shoes."

"I can't go traipsing around outside in a nightgown."

He took both her hands and pulled her up. "No one's going to see you except me."

Now pressed against him, the thin cotton the only barrier between her breasts and solid man, she shivered. "Are you sure?"

He brushed a kiss over her forehead. "I'm sure."

"Okay." She slipped on her canvas sneakers and took the hand he offered, allowing him to lead her down the stairs, out the back door and to who knew where else.

The area was dimly lit by moonlight as they headed up a path not wide enough for them to walk side by side. Drew kept hold of her hand and tugged her along behind him at a steady pace. A slight breeze rustled through the trees and an occasional limb grabbed Kristina's ankle. She momentarily considered that she might encounter some poison oak. Nothing like spending the weekend scratching. But her current itch was one she wanted Drew to scratch, and that took precedence over her concerns.

"Where are we going?" she asked in a whisper. "Back to Chicago?"

"It's a swimming hole," he said over one shoulder. "Nice and secluded. We're almost there."

They reached a break in the woods and Kristina came to his side to survey the scene. Immediately before them a dock stretched out over a small cove of water illuminated by a swath of moonlight. Serenity at its finest. A beautiful scene that should be immortalized on a postcard, Kristina decided.

She smiled at Drew and said wistfully, "This is heaven."

He grinned. "Yeah, and I plan to enjoy it to the fullest."

Without warning, Drew released her hand and began stripping while Kristina stood, mouth gaping. He kicked off his deck shoes and divested himself of all clothing, then ran to the end of the dock and dove in. The splash and Drew's shout echoed over the water, yanking Kristina out of her daze.

Wrapping her arms around her waist, she strolled onto the dock, peeking over the end to see Drew immediately beneath. Luckily the water came to his chest, and she couldn't see anything beyond that. Not that she wasn't mildly curious. Okay, *mildly* wasn't exactly sufficient. Unfortunately, Drew had undressed so quickly that Kristina hadn't been given the chance to satisfy that curiosity.

"Come on in," he said, treading water beneath her. "Feels great."

She imagined he would. "From the way you yelled, you could've fooled me. I wouldn't be surprised if you woke the entire household."

"Nah. They're all sound sleepers."

Not quite willing to strip beyond her shoes, Kristina toed out of her sneakers and sat on the end of the wooden pier to dangle her bare feet over the edge.

Drew continued to tread water below her, his wet hair

glistening in the moonlight. "Come on, Kristina. Live a little. I'll make sure you don't drown."

"I used to be a lifeguard," she said. However, she was a little worried about drowning in Drew's sensuality. And for goodness sake, he was naked. She certainly couldn't ignore that if she decided to take the plunge.

He moved closer until he was immediately below her. "Then what are you afraid of?"

"Snakes," she blurted out.

"There's only one you'll have to deal with."

Wonderful. "Poisonous?"

"Not really." His teeth flashed white in the darkness. "It's known as the Connelly Crawler."

Kristina giggled from self-consciousness, from awareness that she was no match for that particular species. "Now, that sounds dangerous."

"Only if he's provoked."

"And what provokes him?"

"Beautiful women."

She turned her attention from Drew to her hands clasped tightly in her lap. The familiar insecurity resurfaced. "Then I guess we don't have to worry, do we?"

Drew tugged on her ankle. "Actually, since you definitely qualify, we do. But I'll try to keep him under control."

Could Kristina keep her own urges under control, especially with him claiming that she was beautiful? She remembered what Lilly had said about sex, and she'd thought it a good idea at the time, but now she wasn't so sure. She still had too many unanswered questions, too much to consider before giving in to Drew and her own yearnings to be with him in every way possible. "Go ahead and have fun. I'll sit right here."

"I refuse to swim alone, Kristina. Give me your hand. You can help me up."

Help him up? Drew, naked as the day he was born? Was she really ready for that?

"Come on, Kristina," he said, holding out his hand.

Be mature, she told herself. Give him a little boost, and ignore his state of undress. As if she could really do that when confronting his nudity up close and personal.

Closing her eyes, she grabbed Drew's hand but instead of him coming up, she fell in, gown and all.

When the cold water engulfed her from toes to ears, she realized why Drew had yelled. But it wasn't long until she was lifted into Drew's strong arms, blanketed by warmth, firmly planted against him. All of him.

"I've got you," he whispered. "Wrap your legs around my waist."

Dear heavens, she couldn't do *that*, knowing what lurked beneath the water's depths. She seriously doubted that what she felt nudging her belly was any form of fish or snake.

Drew whirled her around until her head began to spin and in order to keep from sinking, she braced her hands tightly on his shoulders and circled her legs around his waist.

"Much better." His voice was rough, seductive.

"At least in water I'm practically weightless," she said. "Otherwise, you might throw out your back."

"Stop it."

Kristina was taken aback by his serious tone. "Stop what?"

"Stop putting yourself down like that."

She glanced away. "Sorry. It's a habit."

"One you need to break."

Oh, if only she could. If only Drew could understand

how many years she had fought to accept her size, the cruelty that had been a part of that battle for acceptance. If only she could believe that it really didn't matter to him.

"You are beautiful," he whispered, his gaze leveled on her breasts outlined in detail beneath the now-transparent, clinging cotton gown.

She lowered her eyes, feeling reticent. "Thank you."

He kept one arm around her back and tipped her chin up with his free hand until she contacted his assessing, crystalline gaze. "I mean it, Kristina. If I didn't think so, I wouldn't be in the shape I'm in right now."

"Are you referring to the Crawler?"

"You bet I am. He's a little agitated at the moment."

Nothing Kristina hadn't already noticed. "Sorry."

He traced his tongue over the shell of her ear. "I'm not sorry. I *am* wondering what I'm going to do about it."

Did he mean for them to make love for the first time here, in the water? Was that possible? *Of course it is, you dummy.*

"Drew, I think—"

"I don't want you to think." He ran one fingertip slightly beneath the modest neckline of the gown. "I want you to take this off. Please."

Speechless, she could only nod her approval.

He reached beneath the water and tugged the material up from where it had settled around her hips. Kristina froze from the fear of him seeing her totally naked except for the plain white panties she wore beneath her gown.

Clinging to Drew's shoulders, she remained very still while he worked the gown above her breasts. As if in a trance, she lifted one arm, then the other, until he had it over her head before she could draw a much-needed breath or issue a protest. Drew tossed the discarded gown and it slapped the surface of the dock with a *plunk.*

He started moving out of deep water, although Kristina still felt as if she were up to her neck in need. "Where are we going?" she asked.

"Closer to the bank so I can see you better."

He kept traveling until the water no longer provided shelter above her waist. Kristina resisted the urge to cover herself, but she couldn't look Drew in the eye.

"You can touch bottom here," he whispered.

She slid her legs down until her toes contacted solid ground, but she still felt dizzy, disoriented, only mildly aware of the night sounds surrounding them. Her focus centered on Drew's strong arms, every place they touched, the faint scent of soap on his skin, the width of his shoulders beneath her grasp. Convening all her courage, she finally raised her eyes to his.

He took a long lingering look at her breasts then sent Kristina a sultry smile that made her flush from head to toe. "You are incredible," he murmured.

Incredible was right. Even though Kristina was standing in cool water, her bare flesh exposed to the nippy night air, a slow, liquid blaze traveled the length of her, creating a riot of desire deep within.

He kept his eyes locked into hers while he gently stroked his thumbs on the sides of her bare breasts, over and over until he had her wanting and waiting for him to go farther. He kissed her then, a hot thrilling kiss that blocked everything but him from her consciousness. All her worries disappeared as if carried away on a current of longing. With each passage of his tongue between her parted lips, she could only consider the way he made her feel—desperate, desired…beautiful.

Slowly he moved his hands to palm her breasts and

Kristina felt as liquid as the water where she now stood. He broke the kiss and his lips came to rest on her neck then slowly slid downward to the valley between her breasts.

Kristina felt totally consumed by the heavenly sensations, and a needy sound escaped her mouth as Drew circled his tongue around her nipple. As if she'd suddenly divorced herself from reality, she slid her hands to his hips and tugged him closer until she could feel every breathtaking part of him.

"I need you, Drew," she whispered. "So much."

Suddenly he raised his head and tipped his forehead against hers. "We probably shouldn't be doing this. We're not ready."

Odd that he hadn't said "*you're* not ready." "I really think I am."

"I'm putting too much pressure on you."

"Why don't you let me be the judge of that?"

He gave her a frustrated look. "I also don't have any condoms with me."

"Then you weren't serious about me getting pregnant?"

His smile was wry. "No, I wasn't serious."

"Not about the laundry or the lawn or the housekeeping either?" she asked hopefully.

"No."

"Then why did you say all those things?"

He glanced away, but not before she saw some unnamed emotion in his eyes. "I was kidding. I thought you realized that."

"Actually, I wasn't sure you were. Not at first." She cupped his jaw in her palm, forcing him to look at her. "But now that I know you so much better, I realize that's not the kind of man you are."

He dropped his arms from around her and stepped back. "You don't know everything about me, Kristina."

Kristina sensed he was about to close himself off again. She wouldn't let him. "I know you love your daughter. I know you've had a hard time since your wife's death. But I also know I can trust you, Drew. I'm beginning to have faith that this relationship could work. Maybe it was even meant to be."

The immediate change in Drew's demeanor indicated that Kristina had said the wrong thing. It was as if someone had flipped a switch and raised an invisible gate, severing any emotional connection they'd shared to this point.

He turned away from her and headed toward the ladder at the side of the dock. "We need to get back before someone realizes we're gone." Once he made it to the top, he kept his back to her while he dressed. "You can wear my shirt. I'll wait for you at the head of the path and we'll walk back together."

Kristina didn't move, even after Drew had slipped on his shorts and shoes and started up the walkway, pausing near the tree line to stare off into the darkness.

Now suffering the effects of the night air and Drew's sudden aloofness, Kristina felt chilled to the bone, and totally helpless. How would she ever break through those barriers he'd built around his heart?

At the moment, that seemed an impossible task. Maybe she should give up. But she couldn't do that. She would have never gotten anywhere in life by throwing in the towel or giving in to the insecurities that still reared their ugly head now and then.

Lilly's advice came back to her, feeding Kristina's determination to try and make Drew forget his pain. Try and prove to him that she was willing to love him with everything she had to give, even if that meant giving him everything, body, soul and heart.

Coward.

Cursing himself and the couch, Drew rolled onto his belly and punched his pillow with the force of his anger. He'd had the perfect opportunity, and he'd blown it.

Kristina had put her faith in him, her trust, and he didn't deserve it one damn bit. Tonight he'd been the ultimate jerk by seducing her, then closing himself off the moment she tried to tell him how she felt about him, how much she admired the man she believed him to be. Funny thing was, she'd mistakenly thought this was about Talia. At one time Talia's death was an issue he hadn't been able to deal with, but since Kristina had come into his life, the guilt and pain were lessening, and he'd begun to feel whole again. Yet he didn't have the guts to tell Kristina the truth, that this scheme to bring them together wasn't his idea at all.

He had told her the truth about one thing. She didn't know him. Not really, even though he'd felt closer to her than any woman, emotionally speaking, since Talia. Maybe even the closest he'd ever felt to a woman, period.

Bottom line, he was lying to her. The whole thing had been a lie. Except tonight he was struck with the realization that he was dangerously close to falling for Kristina Simmons.

That was absolute gospel.

Eight

Kristina's head began to spin as if she were dangling from the massive family tree.

For the past few minutes, Drew's sister-in-law Maura had been seated across from Kristina at the picnic table, attempting to list all of the Connellys, past and present. So far she'd only managed a briefing of Drew's siblings—three sisters and four brothers, including Drew's twin, Brett, not to mention three half brothers. Kristina suspected there was definitely a story there. She could only hope that she wouldn't have to pass a heritage test in order to find her own branch among the tangled limbs, if in fact things worked out between her and Drew. After last night, she wasn't sure she would ever be able to reach past Drew's grief in order to win his heart.

An attractive young woman approached the Connelly men gathered beneath a nearby oak, garnering Kristina's attention. She nodded toward the mystery guest. "Which one is that?"

"She's not a Connelly," Maura said in a whisper. "She's Grant's assistant, Charlotte Masters."

Kristina eyed the woman now conversing with Drew, Grant, Tobias and Maura's physician husband, Doug. She was dressed in a crisp white shirt and neatly pressed navy shorts, while Kristina sat wrapped up to the neck in a modest terry cover-up she wore over her swimsuit. The men seemed more than attentive, and that made Kristina more than a little envious. What red-blooded male could ignore a woman slight of frame with strawberry-blond hair and a striking face? Yet Charlotte didn't smile all that much.

Maura caught Charlotte's attention and signaled her to join them with a wave. "I'll introduce you two."

Charlotte waited for Grant to sign some papers before answering Maura's summons. She strolled to the table to join them, a folder clutched against her chest. Her tentative smile didn't erase the worry from her expression. "Hi, Maura. How are you feeling?"

Maura rubbed a palm over her slightly swollen belly beneath the simple knit top. "Very well, thank you. Would you like something to eat? I'm sure Rosie would be glad to make you a plate. She's just now putting everything away in the kitchen."

"Oh, no. I'm not hungry." The young woman's already pale complexion turned waxen. "Thank you, though."

"Are you feeling okay?" Maura asked.

"Actually, I…" Her gaze wavered for a moment then focused on Kristina.

Maura, too, glanced at Kristina. "I'm sorry. I'm being

rude. Charlotte, this is Drew's fiancée, Kristina Simmons. Soon to be Connelly."

If only that were a concrete fact, Kristina thought. "Nice to meet you, Charlotte."

The young woman's responding smile was pleasant enough, but somewhat distracted. "Very nice to meet you, Kristina."

Feeling as if she were intruding, Kristina asked, "Would you like me to leave so you two can talk?"

"No. That's not necessary." Charlotte sighed. "I suppose there isn't much point in trying to keep it a secret, but I'm not used to...well, having such private matters made public." Her smile was easier, her tone rueful. "I suppose I'd better get used to it, though. I'll be showing soon enough."

Maura's green eyes widened with shock. "You're pregnant?"

"Yes, I am."

The surprised expression remained on Maura's features. "When did you find out?"

"A little while ago," Charlotte said.

A rather vague answer, Kristina decided.

"Sit down and we can exchange war stories," Maura said. "How far along are you?"

Still standing, Charlotte sent a nervous glance at the men who now seemed occupied with their own conversation. "I really can't stay. I need to get back to the office; work doesn't wait, even on Saturday. But since I'm here, I did want to ask you a question. A medical question."

Kristina realized that Charlotte was still evading Maura's questions about how far along she was in the pregnancy, and she wondered if the omission was intentional.

Maura scooted over and patted the bench. "Have a seat for a minute and I'll put on my nurse's cap."

Charlotte reluctantly complied and sat with her hands clasped atop the folder. "Is it normal for me to be having morning sickness all day? Nothing bad actually, I'm just queasy."

"You have been seeing a doctor, haven't you?" Maura asked.

"Oh, yes. But this just started and I haven't had a chance to ask him about it. The thing is, for the last several days I seem to be nauseous all the time. Not severely, but I thought morning sickness only happened when you first woke up."

"What trimester are you in?"

"First."

Finally, an answer, although Kristina still puzzled over Charlotte's obvious avoidance of the question.

Maura laid a hand on Charlotte's arm. "It's perfectly normal, then. I haven't had any morning sickness to speak of, but I was a little light-headed at first. As long as you're keeping food down, consider it one of the little nuisances that comes with bringing a baby into the world."

Kristina decided that a little nuisance now and then would be well worth it, given the opportunity to carry Drew's child. But Charlotte's odd behavior had Kristina wondering if the woman was all that excited about having a baby.

Charlotte slid from the bench and stood. "Thanks, Maura. I need to get back into the office now." She sent Kristina a small smile. "Congratulations, Kristina, and best of luck. Drew's a wonderful man." She left a good deal more quickly than she'd approached them.

"What on earth is up with that woman, racing off that way?"

Kristina looked up to see Lilly standing behind Maura, having returned from inside the house where she'd retired with Emma and Amanda immediately after lunch.

"Actually, she just dropped a bomb," Maura said over one shoulder. "Seems she's pregnant."

"I suspected as much," Lilly said. "I heard her name come up in that context between Grant and Emma. Of course, they didn't realize I was listening."

"You mean you were eavesdropping, Lilly?" Maura asked with mock surprise.

"I was gathering information," Lilly said. "I find it's the only way to keep abreast of the Connelly clan happenings."

"Is Charlotte married?" Kristina asked.

Maura shook her head. "No."

At least now Charlotte's discomfort made more sense to Kristina. She could definitely relate to those times when it seemed the whole world held you under a microscope.

"And as far as I know," Maura added, "she's not involved with anyone."

Lilly expelled an impatient sigh. "I suppose this means you didn't ask about the father."

"I didn't think it was my place to ask," Maura said.

Lilly leaned on her cane and clucked her tongue. "My dear, sometimes being blunt is the only way to discover such an important fact."

"Do you have any idea who this mystery man might be, Lilly?" Kristina asked, genuinely curious.

Lilly carefully slid onto the bench beside Maura. "I haven't a clue. Charlotte has never seemed interested in any of the Connelly sons.'' She rubbed her chin, looking thoughtful. ''Except perhaps Rafe.''

Maura scoffed. ''They argue every time they come in range of each other. Besides, she's not Rafe's type.''

Lilly rolled her eyes. ''I didn't realize Rafe had a type. Just this past year he's dated a dancer, a socialite and a soap-opera star. And wasn't there a tennis player last year?''

Kristina wondered, amused, if Rafe had any idea how well his grandmother kept tabs on his love life.

''But every one of them was definitely a foot-loose-fancy-free sort,'' Maura said. ''I don't see Charlotte that way.''

Looking thoughtful, Lilly said, ''Hmmm. You do have a point. That boy is entirely too skittish about matrimony. Still, he is a man and a Connelly. And Charlotte is an attractive woman.'' She centered her gaze on Kristina and patted her hand. ''Dear, if you're concerned that Drew is a possibility, I assure you that you have nothing to worry about.''

Kristina's face heated to furnace proportions. ''I wasn't actually worried about that.'' Not that the thought hadn't momentarily crossed her mind. After all, Drew had seemed pleased to see Charlotte. And he was a single, vital, gorgeous, sexy man, qualities a woman couldn't easily ignore. Kristina had learned that firsthand.

Lilly and Maura traded knowing smiles, exactly the reason why Kristina avoided playing poker.

The men strolled toward the table and Doug took the empty spot on the bench beside Maura. Tobias slid in on the other side of Lilly while Drew claimed his place next to Kristina, draping an arm around her neck, much to her surprise and joy.

''What were you girls talking about?'' Drew asked.

"Not you, Grandson," Lilly added. "We were discussing Charlotte Masters's pregnancy and the phantom father of her child."

Grant stood in the same spot Charlotte had occupied earlier. "Then she told you."

"She told Kristina and me," Maura said.

Forking a hand through his hair, Grant said, "The secret is now out, but the father still remains a mystery."

Lilly nailed Grant with a serious stare. "I hope it's a mystery to you, Grant Connelly."

"Mother, I'm warning you."

"Oh, posh," Lilly said. "We're all family, and we all know about Seth's parentage. It's not as if it's a secret to Emma, either, God bless your wonderful wife's generous heart."

If only Maura had gotten to Seth in her family summary, Kristina thought. But she hadn't, therefore Kristina couldn't begin to comprehend this conversation. She intended to have Drew explain, if they were ever alone again.

Grant studied the grass beneath his feet. "I would rather not discuss the past, Mother. Emma and I have put all that behind us."

"I'm only saying that I hope you have learned your lesson, my cherished son."

"Let's face it, Grandmother," Doug said, a teasing grin on his handsome face. "Dad's getting a little too old to be dipping into the secretarial pool."

The secretarial pool? Things were becoming all too clear to Kristina.

Lilly cackled. "If a Connelly man's still breathing, he's never too old. This family's males have virility down to a fine art. That certainly still holds true with your grandfather."

Tobias turned red from the tip of his chin to the top of his bald head. "Lilly, behave yourself. You don't want to run Kristina off, do you?"

"Yes, Grandmother, behave yourself," Drew said in a cautionary tone.

Ignoring the warnings, Lilly favored Kristina with a smile. "I'm sure she knows exactly what I mean, don't you, dear?"

"Grandmother, please." Drew's voice was low, barely restrained. His mouth formed a grim line, his eyes devoid of amusement.

"Oh, lighten up, dear Drew. Not one soul here expects you two to be chaste now that you're engaged."

All eyes turned to Kristina as if awaiting confirmation that Drew, like the rest of the Connelly men, had a healthy sexual appetite. She'd only begun to see that side of him, and had to admit she wanted to see more. Soon.

The back door closed, drawing everyone's attention from her, and Emma came out in a flowing blue sundress that matched her eyes. She moved with inherent grace and stopped at her husband's side, slipping her hand into his. Grant and Emma exchanged a meaningful look that could only be described as sincere affection, undisguised love, the way Kristina hoped that Drew might look at her some day.

"Amanda's snoozing away," Emma said. "She told me to wake her when you're ready to go swimming."

Doug rose from the bench. "I'm afraid we're going to have to pass on that swim. I need to get Maura home."

"So soon?" Emma asked.

"I'm afraid so." Maura stretched and yawned. "It's past my nap time." She patted her belly. "Junior here requires lots of rest."

"I could use a little nap, too," Tobias said, patting his belly much the same as Maura had.

"I personally would like a dip in the pool," Lilly added. "But I shall wait until Amanda is up from her nap. Drew, you and Kristina go ahead."

After Maura and Doug had said their goodbyes, Lilly, Tobias, Emma and Grant followed the couple out to their car, leaving Drew and Kristina alone.

Drew pulled his arm from around her and planted his palm on her thigh. "Well?"

"Well what?"

He grazed her bare thigh beneath the terry cloth with light strokes of his fingers. "Care to go for a swim?"

"I'm ready if you are."

He tipped his forehead against her temple and whispered, "Are you?"

Oh, she was. Ready and willing and burning with every brushstroke he made on the inside of her thigh with gentle fingers. "You mean am I ready to swim?" Her voice was little more than a croak.

Drew's smile appeared. "Yeah, I guess so, although you sound like you're ready for something else."

Kristina's face flushed hot. "I think maybe we need to focus on swimming at the moment considering your daughter and grandmother will be joining us in a while."

He nibbled her earlobe. "I could use some cold water right now since it's getting pretty damned hot."

Kristina couldn't argue that. Right now she felt as hot as the coals still smoldering in the nearby barbecue pit. And if he didn't take away his hand, which he'd somehow managed to moved even closer to ground zero, she was going to go up in flames totally.

Clasping his wrist, she said, "The swim, Drew."

With a sigh, Drew pulled his hand back and worked

his way from the bench. "Let's get going before I change my mind and use this table for something other than a picnic."

That image came to Kristina in great detail, bringing with it a slow-burn heat that coursed through her entire body.

Kristina allowed Drew to take her hand and lead her away, but it wasn't on the path they'd navigated the night before. "Isn't the cove the other direction?"

"Yeah, but we're going to the pool."

Kristina laughed. "Probably a good idea. Less chance of encountering snakes."

Drew gave her a smile and her bottom a pat. "Don't count on it, babe. I know one that's already on the alert."

Kristina had no doubt about that. But she didn't understand Drew's sudden change in attitude. Today he was friendly, attentive, quite a contrast from last night. Would she ever be able to read him or understand his moods?

They started down a rock stairway leading to a small cabana that faced the lake. The pool soon came into sight, a large pool with a deck strewn with myriad lounge chairs and tables.

"Very nice," Kristina said once they entered the iron gate.

"It would be if you take off that cover-up."

Again, Kristina felt suddenly shy, ridiculous since Drew had seen her practically naked the night before. But now it was the harsh light of day, and although her swimsuit was relatively modest, she couldn't shake the familiar self-consciousness.

She nodded toward the cabana. "What's in there?"

"I'll show you." Drew tugged her toward the small pool house, released her hand and opened the door, allowing her entry.

Cool air drifted over Kristina as she entered, but it did nothing to quell the heady heat in her body when she turned to find Drew leaning back against the closed door, removing his T-shirt and baring his awe-inspiring chest to Kristina's hungry gaze.

"Your turn," he said in a low command.

Kristina's hands went to the sash tied at her waist. Her fingers trembled, fumbled as she tried to loosen the belt.

Drew pushed off the door and walked toward her with a determined gait that matched his expression. "Let me help."

Kristina really didn't need his help, but she couldn't deny that she wanted it.

Once he had the tie undone, he pushed the garment from her shoulders and it fell to the floor in a pool of terry. When he took a long, lingering look over the suit, Kristina felt self-conscious. She tugged the black tank top lower, though it covered her midriff.

Clasping her wrists, Drew prevented her from doing so. "We'll have none of that, Ms. Simmons. Not until I get a good look at you."

"It's nothing special," she said.

He braced his hands on her hips. "I'd have to disagree. It looks great on you."

Drew worked his palms beneath the tank's hem, pausing at Kristina's rib cage. His hands felt warm against her sides, and she found herself wishing he'd keep going up, up until she saw stars again, this time without the benefit of a night sky.

But he didn't move his hands. He just kept staring at her with an expression that seemed too serious for the moment.

"What's wrong?" Kristina asked.

"I'm sorry about last night," he said. "I didn't want

to make you do something you didn't want to do. I still don't.''

She breezed her hands over the spattering of dark hair on his chest, across his flat brown nipples that peaked beneath her palms. "I don't recall issuing one protest, Mr. Connelly.''

His smile crooked the corners of his magnificent mouth, and his eyes took on a bedroom hue of blue. "Yeah, I guess you're right. But I think maybe we should talk.''

"I'm not in the mood to talk." Kristina draped her arms around his neck and moved flush against him, finding that Drew was very much aroused. So was she. "I stayed awake half the night thinking about us. About how you made me feel.''

"It's only the beginning, Kristina," he murmured. "I can make you feel even better.''

As if he intended to keep that sensual promise, Drew walked her backward until she touched the wall.

"I've never ached like this before," she whispered, pushing away the random lock of dark hair from his forehead now covered with a fine sheen of perspiration.

He whisked a kiss over her cheek then swept one below her ear with lips as delicious and inviting as cotton candy. "Any particular place?''

"Several places," Kristina admitted, her words coming out in a breathy whisper.

Drew slid his hand up under the top to cup her bare breasts in his palms, teasing her nipples with his thumbs. "Here?''

"Yes.''

He trailed one hand down to her abdomen. "How about here?''

"You're getting warmer." So was she.

He moved lower until his palm came to rest between her thighs, the place that ached most for his touch. "Here?"

When she considered what was about to happen, Kristina automatically tensed.

"Do you want me to stop?" he asked, shifting his hand back to her waist.

"No, I— It's just that I— Amanda might show up."

"She's probably still asleep."

In reality, this had nothing to do with Amanda, and everything to do with Kristina's concerns about her own inexperience. "No one's ever— I mean—"

"I know, and I'm not going to hurt you." He brushed a kiss over her lips. "Relax, Kristina. Let me do this for you."

She couldn't relax knowing what Drew had in mind, to satisfy the ache, to touch her in a way no man ever had.

But she melted against Drew when he grazed his tongue across her parted lips then slipped inside her mouth, his fingertips poised beneath the band of the suit's bottoms. He kissed her deeply while he moved his hand lower, and lower still, balanced on the brink of taking their relationship further into the realm of intimacy.

A child's shout broke through the sensual fog clouding Kristina's mind.

Drew took an abrupt step back. "Mandy."

Without another word, he rushed out the door, not bothering to close it, and dove into the pool.

Kristina straightened her suit and patted her cheeks as if that could really remove the blush she knew still existed.

"Kristina! Drew! We have arrived, dear hearts."

Lilly.

Oh, heavens. Kristina would have to face not only Mandy but Drew's grandmother, too. She tried to put on a happy face and meet the challenge head-on, hoping against hope that she could look Lilly in the eye knowing how close Drew had come to showing her pleasure she'd never known before.

Poor Drew, Kristina thought. His problem would definitely be more obvious. She hoped the water was cold enough to tame the serpent.

During his swim, Drew had avoided doing the backstroke, had definitely avoided looking at Kristina or his grandmother. He hadn't been able to avoid thinking about what had almost happened. Five more seconds, and he would have been caught giving Kristina what he knew she needed most, what he definitely wanted to provide.

Now, an hour since they'd left the pool, Drew could only think of how easy it would be to join Kristina in the shower for a different kind of water play. But Mandy and his parents and grandfather were still here, along with his grandmother, who was the only one sitting with him in the great room, conducting a serious survey of his face, gearing up to say something that Drew wasn't sure he wanted to hear.

"We're heading back to the cottage for the night."

Of all things, he hadn't predicted that. "What about the paint fumes?"

Lilly rolled her eyes to the vaulted ceiling. "Oh, good grief. A little paint never hurt anyone. And according to the caretaker, the place is aired out enough for occupants."

"You're all welcome to stay if there's still a problem." Drew's offer sounded less than enthusiastic, and rightfully so. He didn't relish the fact that he couldn't crawl in bed with Kristina if his family was present. Of course, he still couldn't do that. Not with Mandy in the house.

"I only foresee one problem," Lilly said. "And I intend to take care of that."

Here it comes, Drew thought. "What problem?"

"Yours and Kristina's privacy. For that reason, we're going to take Amanda with us."

Drew came to attention and shifted in his chair. "Does Mandy know this?"

"Of course, dear. I told her that you and Kristina need some time alone, and that she and I would spend the evening at Grant's computer. She's more than willing to come along."

"Grandmother—"

"I promise we'll avoid the singles' site. After all, we don't really need that now, do we?"

That reminded Drew of his most pressing concern. "I still haven't told Kristina about this whole scheme."

"Nor should you, dear."

"Don't you think she has a right to know?"

"Perhaps on your golden anniversary. By that time she'll be too tired to issue a protest."

Drew nixed that idea. Somehow, someway, he had to tell Kristina, before someone else did. "I'm worried Mandy's going to slip up and say something. I'm surprised she hasn't already."

"Let me worry about your daughter, Drew. We have an understanding, and quite frankly, I'm not certain she cares how this whole thing came about. She only knows that her father has found the right mate for him and a mother for her."

"It's not that simple, Grandmother."

"Yes, it is that simple. I know you've already opened

your eyes and seen what a truly special woman Kristina is. Now you must open your heart and let her inside."

If only it *were* that simple, Drew thought. But he couldn't disregard the extra emotional load he still carried around. Maybe tonight, when they were alone, truly alone, he could find a way to discard some of that burden.

Lilly braced her hand on the cane and stood when Kristina entered the room. "Feel better after your shower, dear?"

Kristina smiled as she ran a brush through her damp hair. "Much better."

Drew wasn't feeling better at all. Kristina might not be wearing a swimsuit, but the ankle-length knit dress adhered to her breasts and outlined them in great detail. If he didn't get his eyes off her now, he was going to reveal his biggest problem to his grandmother.

"I'm going to check on Amanda," Lilly said, making her way toward the stairs. "She's packing for the trip."

Kristina stopped brushing her hair midstroke. "Are we going home?" Her voice was laced with disappointment.

Drew rose from the chair and shoved his hands into his pockets in an effort to hide his sins. "No. Amanda's going to my parents' lake house with the rest of the family."

Her eyes reflected awareness. "Then you and I are—"

"Going to stay here." He walked to her, but didn't dare touch her. Not now. Not until everyone was safely out of the house and on their way.

"We'll be alone?" she asked, a slight tremor in her voice.

"Yeah. Alone. No interruptions."

There'd be nothing to stop Drew from touching her the

way he wanted, and damn if he didn't want that. But first, he had to decide how he was going to tell her the truth. And after he did that, a good chance existed that she wouldn't want him touching her ever again.

Nine

After having waited for what seemed like a century to get Kristina alone, Drew's stomach coiled into knots of apprehension. Nothing stood in the way of their privacy. Nothing prevented them from being together in every way. Nothing could stop them from making love. Except for the fact that he hadn't come clean about his grandmother's ploy.

He had to tell Kristina the truth. Immediately. Just as soon as she joined him in the great room, where he'd lit the logs in the hearth because during dinner she'd said how romantic that would be. Unfortunately, it was hot as Hades outside, so he'd turned up the air-conditioning, brought out some champagne and waited like a nervous bridegroom for Kristina to make an appearance so he could lower the boom. More like a guillotine, and it seemed dangerously close to his neck.

Still, he had no choice. He'd have to tell her that yeah,

his grandmother had thrown them together. No, he hadn't written the e-mails. No, he hadn't wanted to go along with the scheme. But since she'd come into his life, things had definitely changed. And did it really matter how their meeting had come about? In the long run, what happened from here on out seemed more important than how they'd arrived at this juncture.

Drew couldn't deny he wanted to be with her now. Maybe even longer. Forever? He wasn't sure about that, but he was willing to find out, if she decided to give him a chance after confession time.

He poured himself a glass of champagne and stretched out on his side on the plush, multicolored rug, his feet to the fire. Funny, that was exactly how he felt knowing what he needed to tell Kristina.

The mantel clock counted down the seconds with annoying ticks while Drew tried to mentally rehearse his speech. All he could think about was Kristina, what he wanted to do with her. To her. Although he wore only his pajama bottoms, the heat from the fire was pretty intense. So was the blaze below his belt.

Speaking of heat…

Kristina entered the room wearing the lace gown he'd bought her on his trip to Canada. Sheer lace that left little to his imagination, not that he hadn't already seen her finest features. But the short black gown did things to her body that could easily give a man a cardiac arrest, even one who happened to be less than thirty years old. His internal thermometer rose to dangerous levels, along with the rest of him. He was suddenly balanced on the boiling point, and it had nothing to do with the burning timber.

Kristina kept her eyes lowered as she approached him, looking more than a little self-conscious. If he were a gentleman, he'd stand and greet her, but he didn't dare.

By doing so, he'd risk exposing the fact that he was already revved up and raring to go.

Talking suddenly seemed less than appealing. Right now all he wanted to do was strip away that gown, take her into his arms, and roll her onto the floor so he could finally get inside her. No, he didn't want to talk.

"I think we need to talk, Drew."

Damn. He rose to a sitting position and patted the rug beside him. "Have a seat."

She came to her knees beside him, palms resting on her lace-covered thighs. Drew wanted to put his hands there, too, and higher.

"The fire's nice," she said quietly.

"Yeah. Kind of ridiculous considering the weather, but I guess it does provide a certain ambience." He nodded toward the coffee table where a silver bucket held the bottle of champagne. "Do you want a glass?"

She shook her head, not yet meeting his eyes. "Maybe later. Once we have something to celebrate."

Drew got a sneaking suspicion something was wrong. "What's going on, Kristina?"

She sighed. "I think it's important that we're honest with each other, and that's why I have to tell you what's on my mind."

Surely she wasn't referring to his grandmother's plan? "Okay. Go ahead."

She sighed. "Last night I talked to Lilly about a few things."

Man, she *did* know. "What exactly did she tell you?"

"Details you've managed to avoid since we met."

The weight lifted from Drew's chest, replaced by an astounding relief that the truth was finally out in the open, at least most of it, and she was still here with him. "I can't believe you haven't walked out the door."

She laid a hand on his forearm. "Do you think that learning about the circumstances behind your wife's death would make me up and leave?"

She wanted to talk about Talia? Obviously she still had no idea about the e-mails, but she apparently knew details about his wife's demise. Leave it to Lilly to protect her own secrets, yet have no qualms about revealing his.

"That's all in the past, Kristina. I don't feel like bringing it up tonight."

"I know you don't, but I can't go any further in this relationship until I know I'm not going to continue to compete with your wife's memory."

He frowned. "Is that what you think you've been doing?"

She raised a fine dark brow. "Isn't it?"

Drew grabbed a pillow from the sofa and stretched out on his back. He stared at the ceiling, unsure of how much he was willing to reveal. "I don't know what Lilly told you, but I don't think you understand everything that went on."

"Why don't you make me understand?"

He hated calling up all those bitter memories, hated baring his soul. But Kristina was right, she needed to know about his failures. After learning the details, she probably *would* pack her bags and catch a ride back into the city. Odd, that was exactly what he'd wanted in the beginning, to drive her away, yet now he despised the prospect that she might be out of his life for good.

At least he wouldn't have to worry about how this whole relationship had come into play. He wouldn't have to tell her about the e-mails, or Lilly's scheming. It wouldn't matter how they'd come together since more than likely they'd soon be apart. He hated even thinking about that now.

"What do you want to know?" he asked.

"I guess I'd like to know what you loved about her."

A tough question, one he'd avoided asking himself. "Talia and I were young when we met. You could probably say we started out more in lust than in love."

"Are you saying you didn't love her?"

"I loved her for giving me Mandy, but she didn't love me for that. I got her pregnant and took away her dreams. She couldn't handle it."

Drew glanced at Kristina in an attempt to weigh her reaction. He saw no disapproval in her eyes, only concern. "Did she ever ask if you had any objections to pursuing her career after Mandy was born?"

"No, but I didn't ask. I was too busy with school, working in the family business. Then when Mandy was born, Talia totally withdrew. We didn't talk much. We stopped making love completely. I kept thinking time would make a difference, that she'd eventually settle in to being a mother. It didn't happen."

"She wasn't a good mother?"

Drew noted the distress in her expression. Kristina had natural maternal instincts. She was a born nurturer, so it would be logical that she might not understand Talia's problems. "As I said, Talia was very young. She went through the motions of being a mother, caring for Mandy's basic needs, and I know she really loved her. But the minute I came home, she went to bed, and Mandy was all mine."

Drew recalled those wonderful nights, remembered the way Mandy smelled after he'd bathed her, her tiny cheek resting against his chest when he'd rocked her to sleep, the silly way he'd talked and her responding baby smiles. Great times, until everything had come apart.

"That must have been a huge burden, caring for a

child on top of all your responsibilities,'' Kristina said, pulling him from the recollections.

"I didn't resent it because I loved Mandy. She always seemed glad to see me. I looked forward to coming home for that reason. But I ignored Talia's depression.''

"Did you find her a doctor?''

"Not at first. Everyone told me, including Talia, that it was just postpartum depression and it would eventually go away. After Mandy was a few months old, Talia didn't get any better so I insisted she see a psychiatrist, which she did. He put her on antidepressants, but they didn't do much good. I called him a couple of times, and he told me it would take a while for her to adjust. She never did.''

A long silence followed until Kristina finally said, "Lilly told me she died from a drug overdose.''

"Prescription drugs. It happened before I came home one night.''

Kristina covered her mouth with one hand, but it didn't stifle the gasp. "You found her?''

"No. Not me.'' This was the part he hated most, the very worst moment of his life. "When Talia's mother couldn't reach her, or me, she called the neighbors. They called the police. By the time I got home, the paramedics were there, working on her. I found Mandy sitting in the playpen. I could tell she'd been crying for God only knows how long. She was just a baby.''

The scene played out in Drew's mind with great detail, calling up a wrenching pain in his heart that never went away, even after all this time. "I still remember her sobs, how she looked up at me and opened her arms and laughed through her tears, as if I were some knight coming to her rescue. I just sat on the floor and held her. I didn't know what else to do. I didn't want to let her go because she was so afraid, and I knew I should probably be seeing to Talia. It was a nightmare.''

Kristina gently touched his face. "Oh, Drew. I'm so sorry.''

He swallowed around the painful knot in his throat. "I still feel like it was all my fault. If I had been more adamant, gone to see her doctor and made him understand that Talia wasn't getting any better, then maybe it wouldn't have happened. If I had been home earlier. If I had been more careful and not gotten her pregnant—''

"Then you wouldn't have Amanda now.''

Drew lowered his eyes. "No, I wouldn't. But I worry that this will somehow affect Mandy later down the road.''

"Children are resilient, Drew. She seems very well-adjusted, and she has you to thank for that. She knows how much you love her. That love has sustained her, gotten her past the crisis. She'll only remember what a wonderful father you've been to her.''

If only he could believe so strongly in the power of love. If only he could open himself up enough to give Kristina that kind of love, the commitment she deserved. In reality, he had opened up to her, more than he had to anyone and his burden felt much lighter, even if not completely diminished.

She stretched out and faced him then ran a gentle hand over his jaw. "You were young and had the responsibility of a child, making a living, and a wife who was ill. Talia's death was horrible and tragic, but it wasn't your fault.''

He really wanted to believe that, but the mistakes still ate at him. "I took too many wrong turns. I wasn't strong enough to keep her afloat.''

"You did what you thought was best and the rest was

up to her. Even if you could go back and change things, that doesn't mean it would turn out any differently. It was beyond your control.''

''But I keep wondering—''

She stopped his words with a soft kiss. ''Don't wonder, Drew. You're only torturing yourself. It's time to put it all behind you. It's done. And just because you have made a few mistakes doesn't make you any less of a man. You're a wonderful, caring man and father.''

Drew saw compassion reflecting in her beautiful brown eyes, and admiration. For him. ''I don't deserve you, Kristina.''

''I disagree. We both deserve to be happy, beginning tonight.''

Kristina rose to her feet and worked the thin straps off her shoulders. The gown fell to the floor, leaving her completely naked, allowing him to take a long visual journey down her body. Her slight tremble was the only indication of discomfort, very unlike the woman who'd barely been able to look at him that first day they'd met. She seemed more secure in her appearance, and she had every right to be considering she could qualify as a goddess with her generous curves, her incredible breasts, her smooth skin that made him want to send his mouth over every inch of her.

''Come here, lady,'' he said as he held out his hand. ''I plan to make you very happy tonight.'' Not only tonight, but in the days to come. The months to come. Maybe even the years to come.

Kristina joined him again, this time in his arms. She kissed him first, a deep, satisfying kiss that echoed the emotions rising inside him from a place he'd buried beneath guilt. A guilt that had lessened because of Kristina—a remarkable woman, forgiving, insightful, sensual.

As he explored the reaches of her warm, wet mouth with his tongue, he traveled along her feminine lines with hungry hands, discovering, memorizing, wanting. Then he rose above her and stared into her eyes as he palmed her breast.

"You are so incredible, Kristina," he murmured. "All of you. I want you more than I've ever wanted any woman." Even Talia, because this was different. What he glimpsed in Kristina's eyes was more than lust, more than he'd ever believed possible. It was love in its purest form, unconcerned with past transgressions, unconditional. All for him.

"I love you, Drew," she whispered, her cheeks dampened by tears he intended to kiss away.

She loved him?

He had no idea how he'd managed that kind of commitment from her, but he valued her love more than she knew. And he was going to show her exactly how much.

When Drew stood, Kristina feared he was about to change his mind. Had she been too quick in her admission? Too insistent that he needed to get on with his life? But she wanted him to forget his past, at least tonight, and remember her. If only he would give them a chance to make new memories.

He hovered above her in silence, stared at her with an intense gaze, and she felt totally exposed, body and soul. "Don't," he commanded when she tried to cross her arms over her breasts. "I want to look at you in the firelight. Just for a minute. Then I'm taking you to bed."

Feeling buoyed and brave and bold, she stretched out on her back and toyed with the tiny heart necklace at her throat. Drew's gaze followed her fingertips as she traced a path down the cleft of her breasts, then on to her navel to draw slow circles around the perimeter. She turned to

her side and settled a hand on her hip. He watched her
with darkened eyes as she made brief passes toward the
tangle of curls sheltering secrets she wanted him to uncover with his own capable hands. When her gaze came
to rest below the waistband of his pajamas, she had no
doubt that her blatant demonstration of a woman in need
had fully aroused him. Her nerve endings burned, and a
rush of hot dampness settled between her thighs. Never
before had she believed she could actually do this, become a sensual, uninhibited being. But never before had
she met a man she wanted to do this for.

"Come here."

She accepted his offered hand and found herself pulled
up into his strong arms, melded to his solid body. She
could feel every part of him when he positioned himself
in the cradle of her thighs. His kiss was deep and delving
as he mimicked the act of love with his tongue.

"I'm going to lose it," he murmured, then took her
hand and began pulling her up the stairs behind him. At
the landing, he backed her against the wall and kissed
her again.

He slipped his hand between their bodies and moved
it lower and lower, until it came to rest on her abdomen.
"I can't wait," he murmured. "I don't want you to
wait."

"But the bedroom—"

"In a minute. Right now, enjoy."

And she did, every one of Drew's insistent strokes,
every spark of sensation, every pulse of desire as he
played her like a soothing concerto. She tipped her head
back against the wall as Drew continued his carnal bar-
rage, lost in the retreat and advance of his skilled fingers
deep inside her, then over her sensitive flesh. He suckled

her breast with a gentle pull that created a blissful ache Kristina wasn't sure she could bear without collapsing.

Drew held her tighter and whispered, "You feel so good. Everywhere."

The pressure built and built to a steady crescendo before the climax overtook her, claiming the last of the oxygen from her lungs. She moaned with the pleasure she'd only imagined until now. Her body felt boneless, her knees shaky. Yet Drew was there, holding her, telling her again and again how much he wanted her.

He gave her a few minutes to recover before he led her into his bedroom lit by the bedside lamp, and lowered them onto the bed. The ceiling fan whirling above them did nothing to stop the heat in Kristina's body, the ever-present need she knew would be there until she had all of Drew. She didn't even have the desire to turn off the lights, because she still had much she wanted to see.

Reclaiming her courage, she pushed Drew onto his back and pulled the drawstring at his waist. He lifted his hips, allowing her to work the pajama bottoms down his well-toned legs. She tossed them behind her, and her attention was drawn to a part of him not at all easy to ignore. Taking a slow breath and a long look, she stared in awe, amazed that she had done *that* to him. But considering what he'd done to her, she figured turnabout was definitely fair play.

"Don't be afraid to touch."

Kristina glanced up to find Drew grinning, his hands stacked behind his head. He looked pleased and proud. He had much to be proud of, she decided.

Biting her lip, Kristina reached out her hand and started with a tentative fingertip down his ample length. The hiss of his breath startled Kristina and she pulled her hand back.

"Did I hurt you?" she asked.

"Not even close." His eyes closed tightly. "You have exceptional hands."

"Think so?" She took him into those exceptional hands to stroke and caress, learn and enlighten herself on all that made Drew Connelly the quintessential male.

"That's enough," he said, followed by a ragged breath.

She stroked him once more just in case. "Are you positive?"

With the agility of a pouncing tiger, he had her on her back in record time. He gave her a smile that promised pleasure, sending her whole body reeling with the force of her need. "I'm going to be very careful with you, Kristina."

She really didn't want careful. She wanted hard and lusty. "In case you haven't noticed, I'm not fragile."

"But you haven't been with anyone, and this might hurt a little."

She'd more than gladly take the pain in exchange for the pleasure. "I can handle it, Drew. I promise."

"I don't doubt you can, but I'm still going to be careful."

He left her for a time to retrieve a condom from the nightstand. How convenient, Kristina thought, then admonished herself for giving in to the spark of jealousy. What Drew did before her, and with whom, didn't matter. What he did from this point forward would be her only concern.

And boy, what he did at that moment forced every reasonable thought from her brain. He touched her again and again, brought her back to the brink of climax then positioned himself between her thighs. He kept his eyes focused on hers as he slipped inside, slowly at first, then pushed harder. She concentrated on him, his assessing blue eyes, until the sharp sting of pain came about as he seated himself deeper.

"Breathe, Kristina," he said.

Funny, she hadn't noticed she was holding her breath. She inhaled slowly and exhaled even slower.

"Better?" he asked in a tone that sounded as if he were battling restraint.

She managed a smile. "I'm okay. How about you?"

His responding grin looked almost pained. "I'm great."

"But you will be better in a minute, right?"

"Right."

Feeling brave, she lifted her hips and drew him farther into her body. He sucked in a labored breath. "You're determined to do me in, aren't you?"

"Well, I certainly hope so."

"I'm definitely going to return the favor."

Thrilled by that fact, Kristina clung to his back and prepared for the ride of her life.

Drew didn't disappoint her. Although he was very gentle at first, he seemed to lose control after a time, but then so did Kristina. Total control. They caught a rhythm, their bodies in sync, their limbs intertwined, bare skin meshed together creating slick dampness everywhere they touched. Drew kissed her again, touched her again, brought her to a feverish release again. He shuddered in her arms then tensed when his own climax claimed him. Kristina relished all the sensations, the weight of his body on hers, the strength of his arms.

"You okay, sweetheart?"

Sweetheart? Kristina's heart took flight at the endearment. "I couldn't be better."

He painted soft kisses over her cheeks. "Neither could

I. In fact, I don't know when I've ever felt so good.'' He paused as if he wanted to say something, then added, ''And thirsty. Care for some champagne?''

At the moment, champagne wasn't what she wanted, or needed. She wanted to be held, needed Drew to tell her that what they'd shared had been more than simply ''good.'' At least it had been more for her. So much more.

She recalled what Lilly had said about men and sex and emotions. Maybe now that they'd taken that ultimate step, at some point in time Drew might learn to love her, too. She didn't want to rush him, fearing that by doing so she might drive him away. She had to be patient.

''Champagne sounds great,'' she said, resigned to the fact that Drew was more interested in libations than lingering embraces and love talk. ''Do you want me to go get it?''

''No. I want us to go get it together. Why waste a good fire? I also think we should toast our first evening alone.''

Kristina felt somewhat reassured since he did say their ''first'' evening, meaning he intended there to be more. A very positive sign. ''A toast sounds good, but I'm not sure about the fire. You were sweating like you'd run a marathon when I first walked into the room.''

Drew chuckled. ''That had nothing to do with that fire, babe. Believe me.''

She nipped at his lip, then smoothed her tongue over it. ''Well, maybe we'll cool you off with some champagne. I can certainly think of a few ways to use it.''

He sent her a teasing grin. ''Really? How?''

She brushed a dark lock of hair from his forehead, replacing it with a kiss. ''Oh, I don't know exactly, but it would involve licking it off.''

Drew grinned and patted her bare bottom. "I think I've created a monster."

He had created a woman who for once finally considered herself desirable. A woman who was willing to open her heart to a man whom she trusted with her delicate emotions. A woman completely in love.

Drew fumbled for the annoying phone and answered with "This better be good."

"It is. Really good."

With the receiver clutched in his hand, Drew turned onto his back and sighed. "What's up, Brett?"

"A new Connelly, that's what's up."

Drew could hear the smile in his brother's voice, and couldn't hold back his own grin. "I'll be damned. When?"

"Actually, about ten minutes ago. I called you first since I didn't want to wake everyone yet."

Drew's glance shot to the bedside clock. 7:00 a.m. Way too early, but babies didn't care about time. He'd learned that when Amanda had arrived at 3:00 a.m. on a Sunday, right before midterms. Then something else occurred to him. "Didn't Elena still have a few weeks to go with the pregnancy?"

"Yeah, but the baby's fine, thank God. A little small, but she's okay."

That more than relieved Drew. "Does she have a name?"

"Madison Marie Connelly. She's beautiful. Perfect."

Drew stifled a laugh. His brother, the one-time consummate playboy, was totally smitten over a newborn daughter. How well Drew knew that concept, to have your life consumed by such a gift. "Congratulations, Brett. How's Elena?"

"Happy but tired. She did great, even after twelve hours of labor. I started to call Mother but I didn't know how long we'd be here before Elena delivered. Once we arrived at the pivotal moment, it happened pretty fast."

"Think Elena's up for some visitors?"

"Sure. But if you're coming to the hospital, do it today. She'll probably go home tomorrow."

"I'll try to stop by on our way back into the city. I have someone I'd like you to meet."

"Would that be Kristina?"

"You already know about her?"

"Come on, Drew. News of mating and marriage travels at the speed of light in this family. I'm just kind of offended you didn't tell me yourself."

"You had enough on your mind lately." In reality, Drew hadn't told his brother because he'd had no idea the crazy arrangement would work out with Kristina. But he was really beginning to believe it would work, especially after last night when he'd spent hours loving a woman who had changed him so much it was almost scary.

"I'm telling you now, Brett, that she is one great lady. I think you'll really like her."

"If you like her, then I'll like her."

Drew's feelings for Kristina went beyond simple fondness, that much he now realized. Needing to touch her once again, he reached for Kristina and found the space she had occupied last night empty. He aimed to find out where she'd gone.

"I better grab some sleep while I can," Drew told his brother, knowing in fact he really wanted to grab Kristina. "I'll see you this evening."

Drew hung up the phone and sat up in the bed. The sound of the shower in the adjacent bathroom caught his attention, and he figured Kristina was attempting to wash away the remnants of last night's champagne indulgence. Most of the bottle had ended up on their bodies, not in their bellies. He was still sticky in some pretty unusual places. Kristina Simmons not only had exceptional hands, she also had a very gifted mouth.

That woke all of him up, and he sure as heck didn't want to wait for Kristina to come back to bed and take care of his early rising. After all, he'd considered joining her in the shower many times. A really nice fantasy that would be an even better reality.

He slipped out of the bed and paused at the closed bathroom door when he heard Kristina singing. She had a fantastic voice and a body to match. Both were lethal, especially to a guy who'd recently discovered her many talents. He wanted to experience everything she had to offer, although what he'd already learned about Kristina Simmons went far beyond the physical.

She was all that he could ask for in a woman, a mother for his child. A lover. And most importantly, a friend.

He smiled to himself when he considered that just a few short weeks ago, he'd had no intention of becoming engaged. Now engagement wasn't distasteful in the least, thanks to one lady with a good heart, a kind soul and wisdom beyond her years.

Slowly he turned the knob and opened the door. The room was hazy with steam that clouded the mirrored walls and opaque shower doors. He couldn't make out much beyond Kristina's form underneath the spray. Time for a better look.

He opened the shower stall. "Is there room for me?"

She turned with startled eyes and dropped her hands from her hair. "You scared me."

"Sorry, but I heard this woman singing and I couldn't

help but come in and check it out.'' He let his gaze wander over her wet body and lingered in all the places he'd come to appreciate.

She didn't bother to cover herself and instead leaned back against the wall with a sultry smile. ''Does that make me some sort of Pied Piper?''

He spanned the space between them and braced his palms on both sides of her head. ''Guess it does at that.'' Reaching up, he wiped a mound of snowy suds away from her brow. ''Need some help washing?''

''I'm all done,'' she said in a breathy tone.

''Well, I'm not.''

He buried his face in her neck and worked his way down her warm shower-damp flesh until he came to her breasts. He closed his mouth over a nipple and she grabbed hold of his shoulders as if to anchor herself. Lowering to his knees, he clasped her hips with his palms to hold her steady, his tongue now searching more intimate contours, tasting and teasing while she trembled.

She showed her appreciation with small sounds of pleasure, driving him insane with the pure carnality of her raspy voice as she called his name. With another slow foray of his tongue, she shuddered beneath his mouth.

Kristina clawed at his hair when he didn't halt his exploration, and begged him to stop. She wanted him now.

When he realized he didn't have what he needed in the shower to see this through, he stood. ''I'll be right back.''

''Drew,'' she pleaded once again.

''I need a condom,'' he said. Realizing they'd used up the nightstand cache the evening before, he slipped a towel around his hips, hoping to avoid leaving a wet path in the hall on his way to the living room where he'd left a box hidden in a nylon bag. He'd brought them on the off chance that he might actually need them, out of wishful thinking, and was he ever glad his wish had come true.

Drew yanked open the bedroom door and pulled up short, the towel fisted in a death grip, expecting his mouth to hit the floor at any moment. Better his bottom lip than the towel.

Lilly leaned on her cane and inclined her head. "So sorry to interrupt your shower, dear."

Not as sorry as he was. "What are you doing here?"

She nodded toward the stairwell. "Amanda wanted to see Kristina. She's downstairs having cereal with Grandpa Toby."

"You could've knocked. Or called."

"For your information, I did knock, with my cane. Several times. I tried to call, but the line was busy. I assumed you and Kristina would still be sleeping."

"We were asleep until Brett called. Elena had her baby."

Lilly smiled. "I know. I spoke with him right before we left. Wonderful news indeed. There's nothing quite like having a new baby in the family, is there? Of course, creating that new life is wonderful as well. Speaking of that…" She leaned around him to peer through the open door. "Where is Kristina?"

He yanked the door closed behind him, yet had no desire to beat around the bush, or to spare his grandmother's delicate sensibilities, not that she had any. "She's in the shower."

Lilly's knowing smile bordered on devilish. "How nice that you decided to conserve water." She turned away and said, "I'll keep Miss Amanda company until you are properly bathed and attired." She paused and glanced over one shoulder. "Will an hour be enough time?"

Considering his recent condition, five minutes might suffice. Or it would have had she not shown up. Nothing like encountering your grandmother to quell carnal urges. "We'll be down in a few minutes."

She pivoted around with more agility than most people half her age. "Oh, don't rush on my account. We'll keep your daughter occupied. In fact, I suggest that while you're finishing up, you might start planning your nuptials. I believe you've already taken care of the honeymoon."

She hobbled down the stairs before Drew could arrive at a proper comeback. He hoped that Lilly didn't come back until he'd finished his shower, unfortunately without Kristina.

Ten

Drew arrived at the hospital that evening without Kristina who'd insisted on staying at home with his overly tired and irritable daughter. She'd assured Drew that other opportunities would arise to meet Brett and Elena when Mandy was more rested.

A good idea for many reasons, Drew decided. He wanted a few moments to talk to Brett and seek his brother's advice on how to handle telling Kristina the truth.

At the room, Drew rapped on the door, and Brett greeted him with a tiny pink bundle curled in the crook of his arm. "What have you got there?" Drew asked, lowering his voice when he noticed Elena sleeping in the nearby bed.

Brett opened the blanket, revealing a tiny dark-haired baby with her hands fisted beneath her chin. The good memories came back to Drew, memories of Mandy as a baby, although it seemed ages ago when she was so small, so dependent on him for everything. Each passing day brought with it Mandy's quest for independence, a hard thing to deal with, but inevitable.

"Isn't she the best-looking baby you've ever seen?" Brett whispered.

Drew sent him an answering smile, thinking that all new fathers believed they alone set the standard for quality kids. He'd felt the same about his own daughter. He still did. "One fine-looking little lady."

Brett carefully laid the baby in the portable crib near the hospital bed then gestured toward the hall.

Drew joined his brother outside the door and offered his hand. "You've got a keeper, bro."

Brett grinned. "Yeah, that she is. Hope you don't mind that I didn't wake Elena, but she's just now gone to sleep."

"No problem. Labor's tough on a woman."

"Not too easy on the man, either. There were times I felt pretty helpless."

"I know what you mean."

Brett's smiled faded. "Guess you do at that. So where's your new lady?"

"Home with Mandy who was a bear on the drive back in from the lake. Kristina told me to give you her best and she looks forward to meeting you after you're home with the new family."

"I'm looking forward to it, too." Brett eyed him curiously. "I guess congratulations are in order now that you've decided to tie the knot again."

"That's what I wanted to talk with you about." Drew studied the tile floor, gathering his thoughts.

"Trouble in paradise already?"

Drew's gaze shot to his brother, although he wasn't

surprised that Brett sensed his discomfort. That innate bond had existed between them since childhood. "Actually, it's better than I expected. Better than I'd ever hoped for."

"Then what's the problem?"

"Lilly."

Brett frowned. "What does Grandmother have to do with this? Are you saying she doesn't approve of your woman?"

Drew barked a laugh. "Oh, she approves, all right. As a matter of fact, she's responsible for this whole engagement."

"You mean Grandmother fixed you up?"

"Yeah, so to speak. She found Kristina on an Internet singles' site while I was in Europe. We were the perfect match, she said."

"And you don't agree?"

"Yeah, I do. But there's a big problem."

At Brett's totally confused expression, Drew went on, "Grandmother sent all the e-mails, pretending to be me. She even had Mandy in on the act. Odd thing is, I had no intention of keeping this charade going. At first I didn't want to hurt Kristina's feelings, so I decided to try and discourage her. But now—"

"You've fallen in love with her?"

"I think maybe I have." Drew surprised himself with the ease of the admission, but he couldn't deny the fact any longer. He did love Kristina, everything about her. That realization had hit him the night before, when they'd made love. But admittedly, it had scared the hell out of him, so he hadn't bothered to tell her. But he needed to tell her, and soon.

Brett rubbed his shadowed jaw and sighed. "Kristina has no idea what transpired up to your meeting?"

"No, and I don't k
to blow away all her
Brett patted Drew'
When it comes right
how this all began.
prime example. Mad
but I started to think

Drew admired Br
bility for a child th
nation before they
shouldn't matter ho
together now, and t

"Have you told
"Not yet. I'm n
"Then that's wl
in the words *I love*
rest will work itse

If only Drew c
sounded. "You re

"You bet I do.
always grovel."

Drew and Bret
shrill baby cry cc

Brett nodded
cue."

"Go ahead,"
when you all ge

Brett paused
sure to bring K
finally pulled y

"I hope you

Smiling, Bre
And good luck

Drew believ

She cou
continue th
How car
Was her
that were
about it. S
wasn't desp
been, a last
fortunately,

"I can't
me."

Drew had
met with Ki

"Tell you
the answer.

Kristina s
plain cotton
folded tightl
about some
front of the
ones your gi

Drew felt
a speeding c

"Your dau
He had no
have told yo

"And why
"I tried. I
door, but you

"And you
laugh. "Poor
resorted to a
stamped on n

dn't understand what had motivated him to
 pretense. Fear? Or pity?

you keep a man unless you lose some weight?
mother right? Did Drew feel sorry for her? If
he case, Kristina would have plenty to say
e might not be every man's ideal, but she
erate. Drew Connelly was not, and never had
-ditch attempt to find a suitable partner. Un-
he was the man she loved with all her heart.

believe you didn't have the decency to tell

barely stepped into the den before he was
istina's stern words and stony expression.
 what?'' he asked, although he already knew

trolled around the room, still wearing the
 shirt and shorts from that day, her arms
y over her chest. "Oh, just a little matter
-mails. You know the ones." She paused in
ofa and nailed him with an icy stare. "The
andmother wrote to me."
as if he were heading toward a brick wall in
r with no brakes. "How did you find out?"
ghter told me. You should have."
 argument for that. "You're right. I should
 in the beginning."
 didn't you?"
meant to that morning you showed up at the
 looked so unsure—"
 felt sorry for me." She released a cynical
 Kristina who couldn't get a man so she
 cyber deal. I might as well have *sucker*
y forehead."

Drew had expected her anger, maybe even expected tears. But he saw no tears, only fury flashing from her dark eyes. "That's not what I thought. I was concerned about hurting your feelings, but then after I got to know you, I realized that it hadn't been such a bad idea after all."

"Stop it, Drew. Stop the lies. You pitied me, so you played along thinking you'd find some way to discourage me. You're still playing along. But I have to admit, the list was very creative."

Drew inwardly flinched at her acid tone even though he couldn't fault her for hating him now. "Yeah, that's what I'd originally planned. But things started to change after a while. I started to change."

"Into what? A trustworthy man? I don't think so."

"If you'll just let me explain—"

"It's a bit late for that, wouldn't you say?"

Drew couldn't remember the last time he'd felt so damned helpless. "Look, I wasn't sure if I would be the right man for you. I didn't think I could give you what you need beyond—"

"Sex?" She gave him a hard look. "Which brings me to another question. Last night, was that more of your charity?"

At that moment, he hated that he hadn't found the courage to tell her how he felt about her when she might have listened. Right now she was too hurt to hear what he was saying. "God, no, Kristina. I wouldn't have made love to you out of pity."

"We had sex, Drew. Lovemaking comes when love is involved."

"But, Kristina, I do care about you. I—"

"You don't know the first thing about caring." She propped a hand on her hip and glared at him. "If you really cared about me, you would have told me sooner, before I..." Her words trailed off and she pinched the bridge of her nose, Drew assumed to stop the tears she seemed so determined to avoid.

Feeling helpless, he strode to her and braced his palms on her shoulders, bent on having his say. She stiffened and fisted her hands at her sides. "Don't...touch...me."

She might as well have delivered a right hook to his jaw. He released her and stepped back. "Look, Kristina, you're tired. We can talk about this in the morning."

Her bottom lip trembled, the first sign that her emotions were about to get the upper hand. But she tipped her chin up and said, "I'm all through talking to you. I'll leave first thing in the morning."

Blind panic pushed the air from his lungs. He was losing her, had already lost her. "You can't just leave like that. Mandy will be devastated." And so would he, but he couldn't make the words form. She wouldn't want to hear it anyway, at least not now. Maybe after she had time to think, she would be more open to hearing him out.

He sighed. "We need you, Kristina."

Her expression softened some. "I can't be an afterthought, Drew. And I have considered how this will affect Amanda. She shouldn't have to suffer because of our mistakes. That's why I would like to continue to give her piano lessons."

At least it was a start. At least then he might be able to convince her how important she was to him, and not because she loved his daughter. Because she loved him, or at least she had before he screwed everything up by not being honest. "I think giving her lessons is a great idea."

"On one condition."

"What's that?"

"I'll teach her during the day, while you're at work. I don't want to see you."

He had totally destroyed her with his carelessness. Totally destroyed any hope of a future with her. He felt defeated, wasted. "If that's what you want."

"It is." She turned away and headed toward the hall, but paused and faced him again, her heart in her beautiful brown eyes. "One other thing. I prefer you tell your family that the breakup was my idea. I don't want them knowing the truth about your deception or Lilly's."

Kristina was thinking about his and his grandmother's reputation at the expense of her own. Another reminder of her goodness, and exactly what he would be losing if he couldn't convince her to give him one more chance.

When she turned away again, Drew called, "Kristina, wait."

She responded with "What?" but didn't afford him even a glance over her shoulder.

He wanted to tell her how much she meant to him, that he had fallen in love with her, intended or not. The words lodged in his throat. After what he'd done to her, they would sound false no matter how sincere the sentiment. Instead, he said the only thing he could think to say. "I'm sorry. For everything."

"So am I," she said, her voice laced with tears. "I'm especially sorry I fell in love with you."

With that, she disappeared into the hall, leaving Drew alone with his guilt, the familiar sorrow as his only companion.

The anger came with the force of a jackhammer, and he aimed it at the coffee table, clearing away the magazines and knickknacks with one sweep of his arm. He felt no better for his tantrum, so he headed for the phone, determined to vent his anger on the woman who had caused this whole mess.

When Lilly answered, he lowered his voice and kept a tight rein on his temper in deference to her station in his family, but he was no less angry with her. "Grand-mother. At my house, 7:00 a.m. on the dot. Be here."

He wasn't going to give up on Kristina without a fight, even if that meant recruiting his grandmother into the battle. After all, this was her doing. All of it.

No matter what happened, he would forever be grateful to Lilly for bringing Kristina into his life. Now if he could only convince Kristina to stay.

Kristina packed the last of her things and set the suit-cases by the bedroom door. Before she left the room, she returned to the bathroom and splashed cold water on her face. Regardless, her eyes were still red rimmed from hours of crying and no sleep. She imagined she would spend several weeks, maybe even months, nursing her wounds.

Luckily her friend Tori had offered to share her apart-ment until Kristina could find another place of her own. But after living in a house that she had begun to consider her home, any place would seem terribly empty, even in the company of her best friend. Still, she had no choice. She wouldn't stay with a man who pitied her. She wanted more than that. She deserved more than that.

Gathering the suitcases, Kristina moved sluggishly into the hall and paused at Amanda's room. She nudged the door open with her elbow just so she could take a mo-ment to study the little girl whom she loved as much as if she were her own.

She didn't want to wake Mandy to deliver the news. She needed time to consider how she would tell her. Tonight she would return and have a talk with Mandy, try to explain, as long as Drew agreed to vacate the premises. Though she had failed to say an actual goodbye to him last night, her message had been loud and clear. She couldn't stay involved in his life if she couldn't trust him, trust his motives.

Moving down the stairs, she heard voices coming from the den, surprised that Drew would have a visitor so early in the morning. She remembered that Tobias had been there that first morning, and she wondered if he'd stopped by. She also wondered what Drew would tell his grandfather, or if perhaps he already knew. She couldn't worry about that now.

Drawing in a cleansing breath, Kristina started down the stairs. But Tobias wasn't the mystery guest. Lilly, her bright blue eyes full of remorse, waited at the bottom landing.

"Hello, Lilly," Kristina said politely, unsure of what to do or say next.

"Good morning, dear. I'm pleased that I've caught you before your departure."

Kristina set her bags at her feet, deciding to give Lilly a few moments of her time. Regardless of what the woman had done, Kristina couldn't help but believe that Lilly's scheme had come from well-meaning intentions, even if it had been deceitful.

Lilly leaned heavily on her cane, then sighed. "I suppose there's not much I can say to convince you how very sorry I am. Perhaps grandmother doesn't always know best."

Kristina shrugged. "It's done, Lilly. All's forgiven."

"Yet you haven't forgiven my grandson."

"I'll forgive him in time," Kristina said. "But I can't forget his dishonesty. I can't trust him."

"Oh, but you can trust him, Kristina. You can trust that he's sitting in the den with a heartache the size of Lake Michigan. He's been up all night trying to find some way to convince you to stay."

"I can't, Lilly. I refuse to be tied to a man who has me in his life because he pities me."

Lilly's features went stern. "He has you in his life because he loves you. Because you have brought him his life back."

If only that were true. "He's never said he loves me."

Lilly rested a gentle hand on Kristina's arm. "You haven't given him a chance."

"I've given him more than enough chances."

"Give him one more."

Emotions warred within Kristina. She so wanted to hear the words, but she feared they might not come. Or worse, he might not mean them. "Even if he does say it, how do I know I can believe him?"

Lilly studied her with wise eyes. "Listen with your heart, Kristina. Then you'll know."

"I don't think I can."

"Certainly you can, my dear. Everyone deserves a second chance." Lilly gestured toward the den. "Now go and let him have his say. If you're not thoroughly convinced that his heart is breaking, and that he loves you more than anything on God's fair earth, then you are free to go."

Kristina stood frozen, uncertain which road to take. She supposed he did deserve, at the very least, a proper goodbye, no matter how painful that would be.

When Kristina started away, Lilly's soft voice came from behind her once again. "Remember to listen with your heart, Kristina."

When Kristina walked into the den, Drew came to his

feet from the sofa. He looked horrible. He hadn't shaved and, in fact, still wore the same clothes he'd had on the night before. The area was littered with debris, as if he'd turned into a human cyclone, tossing things about the room. His eyes were bloodshot and tired, much the same as hers, she supposed.

Kristina stood rigid, determined to hold her ground and not let his distressed demeanor sway her. "Your grandmother said you wanted to see me before I left."

He stood with his hands rooted deep in the pockets of his slacks. "First, I want you to know I didn't ask her here to talk you into staying. I asked her here so I could give her a piece of my mind for starting this whole mess."

Anger and remorse impaled Kristina. Obviously he believed it to be a "mess," not a match made in heaven. "I understand." All too well.

He took a guarded step forward. "I also asked her over to thank her for bringing you into my life."

Admittedly, that lessened her anger, but she still had doubts. "Regardless of what's happened, Drew, I don't regret meeting you, or Amanda."

He hesitated a moment. "Do you really regret loving me?"

Did she? Would she take back the moments they'd shared? Probably not. "It was nice while it lasted."

His expression went from sad to stern. "Dammit, Kristina, does it have to be over?"

"Under the circumstances, I think that's best. You've made it perfectly clear how you—"

"Feel?" He spun away then faced her again with a fierce look. "No I haven't made it at all clear." He released a broken breath and met her gaze. "After Talia died, I gave up on finding someone again. It hurt too badly. But after I met you, for the first time I felt whole again, and willing to take a chance on opening myself up. Maybe I wasn't quite prepared for the transition, but now I am.''

Her resolve began to falter, one doubt at a time. ''Are you really so certain, Drew?''

''I have never been more sure about anything in my life.'' He moved closer until only inches separated them. ''I know that if you walk out that door, I'm going to be faced with more pain, maybe even worse than before. Because this time, I'm more in love than I've ever been. With you, Kristina. All of you. Your smile, your eyes, your beautiful body. Most important, your incredible heart.''

Kristina's lips parted, but nothing came out.

He reached out and touched her face, touched her heart in turn. ''That's right, I said I love you, and I should have told you that days ago when I realized it, but I think I was afraid.''

She spoke around the threatening tears. ''Afraid of what?''

''Afraid that I might not have anything left to give, or that I might let you down.''

He stroked a thumb over her cheek and studied her with sincerity, perhaps with love. ''I'm not afraid anymore, Kristina. I want you in my life from here on out. I want to give you everything you need. I want you to continue your career and I want you as the mother of my child, and all the children we'll make together.''

The tears rolled in a steady stream down Kristina's face, unheeded. Years ago, her instincts had failed her, but had they failed her with Drew? From the moment she'd met him she'd sensed he was a good father, a good man. True, he had been drawn into the scheme against his will and had chosen to perpetuate it because he was a considerate man. He had wanted to let her down easy, and now he was telling her that in the process, he had fallen in love with her.

Maybe their meeting had been unorthodox, but with any relationship came certain challenges. Trust was an issue they would have to work through, if she chose to put her faith in Drew, as she had from the beginning.

Kristina held tight to the last thread of doubt, and then Drew smiled, a smile she had come to cherish each passing day. A smile she wanted to see every day for the rest of her life.

As Lilly had said it would, Kristina's heart spoke to her loud and clear, with love. It told her that this man did love her, despite their questionable beginning. He needed her, and she needed him. They needed to be together.

Kristina rested her palm on Drew's hand, still gently cupping her face. "You don't mean eight children, do you?"

His blue eyes, too, were misty, but his face split into a vibrant grin. "We'll have as many or as few as you'd like. Whatever makes you happy."

She slipped her arms around his waist to hold him close to her body; he already occupied her heart. "You know what would really make me happy?"

He circled his arms around her and pulled her tighter against him. "What?"

"That you'd learn to love wrestling."

He brushed a kiss across her tearstained cheek. "I can do that, as long as you show me a few of your own moves."

He kissed her deeply then, a kiss from the heart, brimming with emotion, with love shared between two people who'd come together in the most unlikely way, only to be together from this day forward.

The sound of a clearing throat caused Drew to break the kiss. Lilly stood near the entrance, Amanda at her side, both looking on with luminous smiles.

"I'm sorry to interrupt," Lilly said. "But I wanted to let you know that Toby and I will be taking Amanda to the zoo."

Mandy rushed into the room and grabbed both Drew and Kristina around the waists. "Is that okay, Daddy?"

Drew bussed the top of Mandy's blond head. "Sure, sweetheart." He winked at Kristina. "We have something we really need to do."

Kristina suspected she knew exactly what he had planned, and she would more than willingly participate.

"I take it everything is settled now, dears?" Lilly asked.

Drew gave his smile to Kristina. "Yeah, I think it is."

"Then it's official?"

Drew frowned at his grandmother. "Official?"

Lilly rolled her eyes. "Oh, good heavens, Drew. Must I do everything for you?"

"Grandmother, you're not making much sense. As usual."

"I'm making perfect sense." Lilly hooked her cane over her forearm and began rummaging through her purse. "I'm speaking of a certain question you should be asking Kristina... Ah, here it is." She handed Drew a small velvet box. "This belonged to my mother. I've waited to pass it on to a granddaughter, but it seemed I was always too late for the proposal. And since Kristina will become my granddaughter, I feel she is most deserving to wear it."

Kristina gasped when Drew opened the box to a sparkling oval diamond centered on a platinum band, larger than anything she'd ever dreamed of wearing.

Lilly tapped Drew's behind with her cane. "On your knees."

Mandy giggled and Kristina froze, thinking the scene had a surreal quality about it. But like any good grandson, Drew lowered himself to one knee, Amanda by his side, and looked up at Kristina with love radiating from his blue eyes.

He held up the ring. "Kristina Simmons, would you do me the honor of being my wife?"

"And being my mommy, too?" Mandy added.

Kristina smiled and fought another rush of tears, this time of joy. "Yes, I would be more than honored."

Drew rose and placed the ring on her finger, then took her into his arms for another kiss, this one more chaste but still as heartfelt as the one before. No longer a trial engagement, their commitment to each other was real.

Kristina looked down when Amanda tugged at the hem of her dress. "What, sweetie?"

"I'm glad you're going to be my mommy since I don't have one anymore."

Kneeling, Kristina said, "Mandy, you do have a mommy. She's just not with you anymore, so I'll be here to help you grow, but I'll never try to take her place."

Drew walked to the bureau, opened a drawer, then returned with a framed photograph. He handed it to his daughter. "This is your mother, Amanda. Like Kristina, she could play the piano. She loved you as much as any mommy could love her daughter."

Amanda studied the picture with awe. "She looks like me, Daddy."

He touched her head. "Yes, sweetheart, she looks like

you. She was very pretty." He glanced at Kristina. "Guess I've gotten lucky twice now."

Kristina felt lucky. Very lucky. This gesture told her that Drew was ready to move on with his life, with her.

Amanda studied the picture a moment longer then handed it back. "Now I have two pretty mommies, Big Daddy."

They all laughed, and as they joined in a group hug—Kristina, Drew, Amanda and Lilly—Kristina realized that families sometimes came together in unusual ways, but the love that would sustain them all came from the heart.

She couldn't have asked for a better beginning.

Once they released each other, Lilly said to Mandy, "Come along, dear heart. Time for the zoo. Your father and Kristina have many plans to make, among other things."

Drew wrapped his arms around Kristina and gave her a lingering kiss. "You two have fun. But remember it's going to be hot today."

"Not as hot as it will be here, I'm sure," Lilly murmured.

Mandy tugged on Drew's hand. "Are we gonna have a big wedding with white dresses?"

He grinned at Mandy. "You bet, sweetheart."

"Oh, Drew," Kristina said. "We don't need to have a big wedding. Small is fine by me."

Lilly cackled. "My dear, you are marrying a Connelly man. They don't know the meaning of small."

"I guess you already know that, huh?" Drew whispered, causing Kristina to blush like a brushfire.

Drew hugged his daughter, then his grandmother. "Thanks, Grandmother. For everything."

Lilly smiled. "My pleasure, beloved. Grandmother always knows best."

In this case, Kristina couldn't agree more.

Epilogue

"Are they really married, Nana Lilly?"

Lilly hugged Amanda close to her heart as they sat behind the banquet table. "Yes, dear, they're really married."

Lilly once had believed that assisting fate was an honorable cause, but, alas, her matchmaking days were over. However, she couldn't stop the tiny nip of pride as she watched her handsome tuxedo-bedecked grandson dance with his new bride, dressed in white Connelly lace, knowing in fact she'd had a hand in this perfect match. At times grandmother did know best, even if some people were hard-pressed to make that concession.

Lilly nudged Amanda from her lap. "Go on, dear heart. Your daddy and Kristina would like you to join them in a dance."

Amanda rushed away in a flurry of pink crinoline skirts and youthful exuberance. Lilly surveyed the room filled almost to capacity with close friends and the Connelly family: Emma and Grant twirling on the ballroom floor along with Maura and Douglas, Elena and Brett, all competing for space as they joined the bride and groom in a waltz.

Lilly noted Tara standing nearby with her intended… what was his name? Ah, yes, John Parker. A nice safe, sensible man who'd recently presented Tara with an extravagant diamond and the promise of a nice, safe, sensible future. Yet this was not a perfect match by any standards; Lilly had realized that the moment Grant had introduced the two. Tara could not love another man the way that she had loved her dear, departed Michael. The way she still loved him. Lilly honestly believed that that certainty, that soul mate, came along only once in a lifetime.

If Lilly had her way, she would have a good sit-down with her granddaughter and try to convince her not to make a snap decision in matters of the heart. But Lilly wouldn't intervene this time. She had barely escaped disaster with her last attempt at facilitating happiness. Tara would have to come to that conclusion on her own.

With her help, everything had worked out grandly with Kristina and Drew, Lilly admitted. Drew had found a woman to heal him, someone he could love through the years, as Lilly had loved her own husband through happiness and heartache.

On that thought, Lilly turned her gaze on Tobias sitting across from her at the table, looking as debonair as he had the day they'd met. He answered her smile with one of his own. No words passed between them, only a timeless love that had existed for five decades.

After blowing Tobias a kiss, Lilly glanced at Drew and Kristina once again, Amanda held securely between them as they waltzed around the floor. Such a wonderful family, indeed. And perhaps soon there would be more children born to the couple to complete their life together, so that they, too, would hold dear to each other, to what they had found together.

One knew in this instance that that would be the case.

* * * * *

DYNASTIES: THE CONNELLYS
continues....
Turn the page for a bonus look at what's in
store for you in the next Connellys book
—only from Silhouette Desire!
THE SECRET BABY BOND
by Cindy Gerard
September 2002

Prologue

For two years, Michael Paige had been a dead man. To some, he was a dead man still. In actuality, not only was he alive, he finally remembered the many things that he'd forgotten.

He remembered what he'd had.

He remembered what he'd lost.

And he wanted it back.

From a distance, from behind dark glasses, he watched Tara—the wife he'd lost even before the world had decided he was dead—while his wildly beating heart reminded him how very much alive he truly was.

Sitting quietly on the park bench, while the early September sun shone brilliant and pure through the shifting oaks and the scent of summer's last roses drifted on the breeze, he watched. And he remembered the way she moved, the way her short, sleek cap of stylish black hair felt sliding like silk between his fingers, the way her vi-

olet eyes clouded to misty lavender when he made love
to her. Two years ago. A lifetime ago.

She smiled, her face full of love for the child who
toddled by her side. The toddler boy wore tiny running
shoes, a baby-size Chicago Cubs jacket and cap and
stared up at his mother through laughing gray eyes.

Through *his* eyes.

A lump formed in his throat that he couldn't swallow.
He had a son.

He had a son whose name was Brandon, whose face
he'd seen and whose name he'd learned for the first time
just two weeks ago. Michael buried his hand in his jacket
pocket and clutched the dog-eared piece of newsprint.
The photo of Tara in the grainy gray print of a tabloid
newspaper had caught his eye in a Quito, Ecuador su-
permarket and blindsided him with a staggering rush of
memory. So had the dramatic account of his own death.

A shooting pain stabbed through his right temple. He
touched two fingers to the scar there and rode it out. It
would pass soon and until it did, he focused on reality.

The reality of his wife. The reality of his son.

An ache swelled and grew and filled his chest with a
love and a longing so profound that he almost went to
the boy then. Just to gather him close. To feel that robust
and healthy little body warm and real against his own.
To look into his liquid silver eyes and see a reflection of
himself there. To cement into fact that the amazing miracle he and Tara had made together was not a cruel trick
of his imagination. And to confirm, unequivocally, that
he really was alive.

But the man who had been Miguel Santiago for the
past two years couldn't do that. Not yet. Not here. So he
stayed where he was and accepted that this was not the
time. This was not the way. He couldn't just walk up to

his child—his child who didn't know him. He couldn't just smile and say to his wife, ''I'm not dead. I was just lost for a while. And I've missed you.''

So he sat, unable to move, unwilling to leave as his son tumbled to his back with a shriek of gurgling laughter—and the man at Tara's side bent to pick him up and lift him into his arms.

Then the three of them walked away together. Tara, his son and the man who would take his place.

It was only after they'd faded to a memory that he realized his hands were clenched into fists inside his pockets, that his eyes were staring blankly.

Michael took one last look at the spot where his wife and son had disappeared. Then he rose and started walking.

This time he promised himself that when he walked, it would be out of the shadows. This time he would walk toward the living, not away.

He wanted his life back.

He wanted his wife back.

He did not want to be dead any longer.

DYNASTIES: THE CONNELLYS

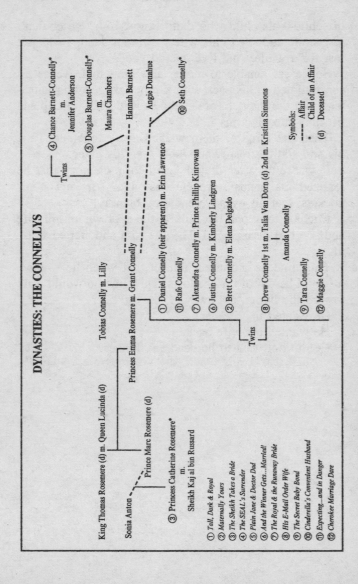

King Thomas Rosemere (d) m. Queen Lucinda (d)

Tobias Connelly m. Lilly

Princess Emma Rosemere m. Grant Connelly

Prince Marc Rosemere (d)

Sonia Anton

Princess Catherine Rosemere*
m.
③ Sheikh Kaj al bin Russard

④ Chance Barnett-Connelly*
m.
Jennifer Anderson

⑤ Douglas Barnett-Connelly*
m.
Maura Chambers

Hannah Barnett

Angie Donahue

⑩ Seth Connelly*

Twins

① Daniel Connelly (heir apparent) m. Erin Lawrence

⑪ Rafe Connelly

⑦ Alexandra Connelly m. Prince Phillip Kinrowan

⑥ Justin Connelly m. Kimberly Lindgren

② Brett Connelly m. Elena Delgado

⑧ Drew Connelly 1st m. Talia Van Dorn (d) 2nd m. Kristina Simmons

Amanda Connelly

⑨ Tara Connelly

⑫ Maggie Connelly

Twins

① Tall, Dark & Royal
② Maternally Yours
③ The Sheikh Takes a Bride
④ The SEAL's Surrender
⑤ Plain Jane & Doctor Dad
⑥ And the Winner Gets...Married!
⑦ The Royal & the Runaway Bride
⑧ His E-Mail Order Wife
⑨ The Secret Baby Bond
⑩ Cinderella's Convenient Husband
⑪ Expecting...and in Danger
⑫ Cherokee Marriage Dare

Symbols:
– – – – Affair
* Child of an Affair
(d) Deceased

presents

A brand-new miniseries about the Connellys of Chicago,
a wealthy, powerful American family tied by blood to the
royal family of the island kingdom of Altaria.
They're wealthy, powerful and rocked by
scandal, betrayal…and passion!

Look for a whole year of glamorous and
utterly romantic tales in 2002:

Where love comes alive™

A powerful earthquake ravages Southern California...

Thousands are trapped beneath the rubble...

The men and women of Morgan Trayhern's team face their most heroic mission yet...

A brand-new series from *USA TODAY* bestselling author

LINDSAY McKENNA

Don't miss these breathtaking stories of the triumph of love!

Look for one title per month from each Silhouette series:

August: THE HEART BENEATH
(Silhouette Special Edition #1486)

September: RIDE THE THUNDER
(Silhouette Desire #1459)

October: THE WILL TO LOVE
(Silhouette Romance #1618)

November: PROTECTING HIS OWN
(Silhouette Intimate Moments #1185)

Available at your favorite retail outlet

Silhouette®

Where love comes alive™

buy books

Your one-stop shop for great reads at great prices. We have all your favorite Harlequin, Silhouette, MIRA and Steeple Hill books, as well as a host of other bestsellers in Other Romances. Discover a wide array of new releases, bargains and hard-to-find books today!

learn to write

Become the writer you always knew you could be: get tips and tools on how to craft the perfect romance novel and have your work critiqued by professional experts in romance fiction. Follow your dream now!

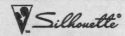

Where love comes alive™—online...

SINTLTW

If you enjoyed what you just read,
then we've got an offer you can't resist!

Take 2 bestselling love stories FREE!

Plus get a FREE surprise gift!

July 2002
IN BLACKHAWK'S BED
#1447 by Barbara McCauley

SECRETS!

Don't miss the latest title in
Barbara McCauley's sizzling and
scandal-filled miniseries.

August 2002
BECKETT'S CINDERELLA
#1453 by Dixie Browning

BECKETT'S FORTUNE

Be sure to check out the first book in
Dixie Browning's exciting crossline
miniseries about two families, four
generations and the one debt that
binds them together!

September 2002
RIDE THE THUNDER
#1459 by Lindsay McKenna

Watch as bestselling author
Lindsay McKenna's sexy mercenaries
battle danger and fight for the hearts
of the women they love, in book two
of her compelling crossline miniseries.

MAN OF THE MONTH

Some men are made for lovin'—and you're sure to love
these three upcoming men of the month!

Available at your favorite retail outlet.

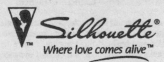

Silhouette®
Where love comes alive™

Visit Silhouette at www.eHarlequin.com   SDMOM02Q3

COMING NEXT MONTH

#1459 RIDE THE THUNDER—Lindsay McKenna
Morgan's Mercenaries: Ultimate Rescue
Lieutenant Nolan Galway didn't believe women belonged in the U.S.
Marines, but then a dangerous mission brought him and former marine pilot
Rhona McGregor together. Though he'd intended to ignore his beautiful copilot,
Nolan soon found himself wanting to surrender to the primitive hunger she
stirred in him....

#1460 THE SECRET BABY BOND—Cindy Gerard
Dynasties: The Connellys
Tara Connelly Paige was stunned when the husband she had thought dead
suddenly reappeared. Michael Paige was still devastatingly handsome, and
she was shaken by her desire for him—body and soul. He claimed he wanted to
be a real husband to her and a father to the son he hadn't known he had. But
could Tara learn to trust him again?

#1461 THE SHERIFF & THE AMNESIAC—Ryanne Corey
As soon as he'd seen her, Sheriff Tyler Cook had known Jenny Kyle was the
soul mate he'd searched for all his life. Her fiery beauty enchanted him, and
when an accident left her with amnesia, he brought her to his home. They soon
succumbed to the attraction smoldering between them, but Tyler wondered what
would happen once Jenny's memory returned....

#1462 PLAIN JANE MACALLISTER—Joan Elliott Pickart
The Baby Bet: The MacAllister Family
A trip home turned Mark Maxwell's life upside down, for he learned that
Emily MacAllister, the woman he'd always loved, had secretly borne him a
son. Hurt and angry, Mark nonetheless vowed to build a relationship with his
son. But his efforts brought him closer to Emily, and his passionate yearning for
her grew. Could they make peace and have their happily-ever-after?

#1463 EXPECTING BRAND'S BABY—Emilie Rose
Because of an inheritance clause, Toni Swenson had to have a baby. She
had a one-night stand with drop-dead-gorgeous cowboy Brand Lander, who
followed her home once he realized she might be carrying his child. When
Brand proposed a marriage of convenience, Toni accepted. And though their
marriage was supposed to be in-name-only, Brand's soul-stirring kisses soon had
Toni wanting the *real* thing....

#1464 THE TYCOON'S LADY—Katherine Garbera
The Bridal Bid
When lovely Angelica Leone fell into his lap at a bachelorette auction, wealthy
businessman Paul Sterling decided she would make the perfect corporate
girlfriend. They settled on a business arrangement of three dates. But Angelica
turned to flame in Paul's arms, and he found himself in danger—of losing his
heart!

SDCNM0802